Linc

discover libraries
This book should be returned on or before the due date.

DONATED BOOK

To renew or order library books please telephone 01522 782010
or visit https://lincolnshirespydus.co.uk
You will require a Personal Identification Number
Ask any member of staff for this.
The above does not apply to Reader's Group Collection Stock.

EC. 199 (LIBS): RS/L5/19

Daniel Frearson

The Last Dragon Slayer Copyright © 2018 by Daniel Frearson.
All Rights Reserved.

ISBN-13 9781718096233

CONTENTS

Prologue 10
1 Heir to the Legend 18
2 History 29
3 The Frist Event 39
4 Containment 53
5 New Tricks 64
6 The Chase 78
7 Control 86
8 White room 96
9 Conference Call 110
10 The Void 122
11 The Second Event 132
12 Protocol 144
13 Subject zero 158
14 Off the Record 168
15 A Swift End 187
16 May Battle Commence 199
17 Final Breaths 213
Epilogue 221

The past can be forgotten, the future can be predicted but the present cannot be permitted to remain ignored.
—DANIEL FREARSON

A brief message

Originally intended as a companion book to The Athereon: Day of Reunion, The Last Dragon Slayer was first written and drafted alongside it. And whilst I was perfectly capable of writing both books at once and had made significant progress into the two by the time that I moved away from this one, I felt that The Athereon necessitated more of my attention as its page count kept growing.

This book was meant to go along side Day of Reunion because it stands as an introduction, backstory and character building piece for one individual character in The Athereon Series.

Whilst having no direct ties to any events detailed in The Athereon Series, this book is undoubtedly still a major part of it. Casting light on topics only mentioned in passing and expanding on truths that play key roles in both the books that came before this one and the ones that will follow; this book cannot be regarded as anything but a key side story to the main Athereon Series.

However I took great care to word discussions well and keep crucial and spoiler related information out of this story as best I could so that any reader who might have chosen to read this book first does not feel as though the rest of the Athereon Series has been ruined for them.

This book can be read at any point in the Athereon Series before Revolution. Reading this after Revolution would be unfortunately repetitive as various events and information mentioned here will have a significant role in that title.

Another important piece of information that I feel that I should disclose is the origin of this story. Or to put it a better way, the lack of it.

Originally I had no set idea in mind when I sat down to start writing this book. Only a character name and role that I wanted him to play. A void in the larger scope of the whole that I needed him to fill. Because of this the entire story beyond this point was made up on the spot as I went and thus led to many extensive rewrites and changes along the way.

At one point I even scrapped the first hundred pages that I had drafted and rewrote the whole thing from the beginning. Keeping in mind the aspects that I had liked and removing those that I had felt were too forced or were out of place.

All in all after the year that I took me to go from my first attempt at drafting this to writing the sentence that you are reading now, this book has gone through many changes. In truth, the original ideas and plot design would have taken this story in such a differing direction that you would be hard pressed to recognise it as the same thing.

For that reason I have chosen to leave this message. The first time that I have ever felt it necessary to do such a thing.

This message is not meant to give warning or excite you for the road ahead. Instead it is meant to inform you. Of why it took so long for me to finally publish this piece and why it might at times read much more differently than my previous work.

This book is the sum of eleven months of thinking and drafting and thus has been reworded greatly as my writing style matured in that time.

From writing this as an intended prequel to Midnight and now as a completely separate story being released during my break from the series; a lot has changed. But rest assured, this book is one of my favourite works not only because I feel that it is my best but because it is one that I myself have had much fun in actually reading.

Never the less, I hope that you enjoy this piece as much if not more than I have in writing it and on behalf of The Athereon himself; we will be seeing you again very soon.

There is still much more of his story to tell.

And so many others that deserve the same.

PROLOGUE

The intermittent pounding thud of the ground that shook the very dirt laid upon it awoke the lone knight lying face first in his own warm blood from his dreamless slumber not a moment too soon.

A black talon no less than four feet in length headed down towards him at speed upon his awakening as the entire front right foot of the beast came down upon him. This beast realising that this knight yet lived and doing its best to eradicate him before he had been given the chance to attack once more.

A deep, almost pitch black claw that was sharper and stronger than hardened steel rushed down through the air with hate fuelled haste and a purely lethal intent within moments of his sudden gasp back to consciousness. And nothing stood in its way to halt it.

Within less than an instant that talon was to come crashing down on the knight, puncturing straight through what remained of his armour and his body before continuing on and penetrating the rock below him as it pinned him down to the ground. Within the time of a single heartbeat, it was surely going to kill him.

That would have been all but certain had he been any ordinary man but the knight in question, had other ideas in mind. He wasn't about to give in so easily. No after all that he had been through already.

His entire body jolted back to life as his eyes finally focused on his target. Turning with such force that he might have broken something from doing it had he been human and flipping over onto his back many times faster than should have been possible.

But once there, staring his impending doom in the face and watching as it approached, his arm rose up towards his soon to be murderer.

Up towards his enemy he pointed his hand. A fist formed on his right side almost instantly and then the glowing power of the jewel attached to it by means of the metal band forming the ring on his finger began radiating from him within an instant.

His will turned to power, his determination, his strength and as his thoughts centred and as this ring interoperated them, it took swift and precise action.

The talon grew closer, coming within an inch of making contact with the man as the time needed for the ring to play its part ticked by and then when it seemed as though he had acted too late – when he believed that he had been incapable of preventing his death; it suddenly stopped in place and moved not a millimetre more than that.

The talon made to be stuck in mid-air, the rest of the foot held in place with it for less an instant before it happened. The foot, the entire leg and body connected to it, bounced back from the knight violently from the force that he had exerted on it. Sending the beast flying through the air away from the severely wounded man on the floor with sufficient force that in place of where it used to stand were now fragments of its own body.

Shards of metal like scale from the beast's hide littering the floor after being ripped and torn from its body from the impactful force applied to it.

The blast of energy that he had barely managed to muster in time, the minute amount of power that he had been able to contain within his hand upon a moment's notice, had not only been enough to save him from the oncoming attack but to harm the beast as well.

Yet one more blow to add to the rest.

Although barely a bruise it might have been; it was still damage. And for one such as him, a human mage, that was greatly impressive. Believing that any mortal could have contained such power was preposterous but to see it happen, to feel it happen, that was unbelievable.

For both the beast and the man whom had harmed it.

The knight sat himself up in an effort to keep up the fight as he had done for hours before then but it was already too late for that. The fight that he had wished to continue, was already lost.

His brothers in arms lay dead and scattered around him. The villagers and the livestock of the neighbouring town that had meant to flee with his protection littered amongst them also.

There was nothing left to fight for now.

He had failed.

And with his right leg broken badly enough to make walking impossible without the immediate attention that he was not in a position to give it, his armour already shredded and his head bleeding heavily from just above the brow; that knight already knew what came next.

He knew that he had no chance of winning.

Even with the powers, knowledge and skill that he possessed, there was nothing that could be done to save him. Not anymore. But that didn't mean that he was finished.

After three hours of tireless conflict, he had been left with no more energy to spare. No more stamina to burn and no more tricks to use. He knew that he was done for, he even accepted it.

Knowing that there were no reinforcements to come even if it had been possible to ask and no way of retreating even if there had been refuge to seek; he was certain that his death awaited him.

The knight who lay on the blood filled dirt below him knew in that instant exactly how grim his situation was. That such a gross and depressing sight was fit for none but the dead. The thing that he was soon to become.

He knew that where he sat in that moment, would be his grave. As it already was for so many others just like him. And that in one way or another, he was to perish there. So he chose in that instant, to go out on his own terms.

And as the beast grew closer once again. Beginning to pick up speed after landing off in the distance in front of him, he knew that he only had one option left.

If he couldn't kill it, if he couldn't stop it, then at the very least he could protect everyone else from it. The ring that he wore and relied on for power was capable of that. He just had to pay the price that it required of him first.

And he was more than willing to go far enough to do just that.

His hand raised once more. A fist pointed at the beast as it scurried towards him and a bright red light illuminating both him and the space surrounding coming from it.

The last of his power was to be placed into it soon enough.

As would his essence and soul.

The potent and unique magic that he had been born with, strengthened and made more accessible through use of the ring that he wore, was to become a part of it.

Forever.

Fused to it as deeply as the gem on its tip.

Empowering it for the generations that would come after him.

A final gift from him and his kind to safeguard the future.

"May god forgive me for what I am about to do." The knight whispered to himself as the time drew near. The beast steadily approaching him as the seconds went by.

Its wings torn and its tale broken. Various cuts and scrapes piercing its thick scales all over its body and with several teeth missing the beast was hardly in the best shape. Not even able to run at full speed as its hind legs struggled to support its weight after such a prolonged period of use.

It wasn't strong enough to keep fighting forever but neither was it weak enough to give in. Not yet.

And neither was the knight.

The two could have continued fighting like that for an hour and they would have been no closer to the end.

That knight hadn't the power to heal himself nor did he have the strength to quell the beast. All he could have done is kept surviving, as he had been doing for much of the fight thus far. So instead, he chose to use that same power in an effort not to win the fight but to put a stop to it.

There was no time to heal himself anyway, no way of making an escape either. He didn't have another choice. He knew beyond any doubt that if he did not do what he was about to then and there, if he were to allow himself to fall, then nothing would survive without him.

The destruction that would follow, could have threatened the entire world. And he could not allow that.

He wasn't ready to give in, nor would he ever be. But at the same time, he had no way of continuing forever. No sure way of winning. Not as long as he was still breathing anyway.

"By the foundation of iron and the core of crystal, I hereby eternally bind this ring." The knight chanted, the radiant glow intensifying, the power within pooling and the dragon instinctively slowing in response to it.

The wind changing direction and condensing around him, the rain ceasing to fall entirely and the rapid lightning spread out for miles above quickly concentrating directly over the knight below it. The sky itself, reacting to the power that he was about to unleash.

The planet itself, realising that what he had planned to do; was starting.

"May it be that for all whom might seek its boundless power, to all whom might gain purpose from its use, I hereby seal this ring!" He continued, the lightning striking down in one powerful blow right in front of the beast approaching him, halting its movement entirely for the briefest of moments as the air pressure changed even more.

A sudden and powerful blast of gushing winds radiating outwards from his position and hitting the beast little by little as they approached. Seeping into its very core as it neared the knight, locking into its scales, its bones and its blood. Fusing the power within it to that of the power effecting it.

Shackling it.

"And for the sake of the people, the land and the future to come, I hereby BANISH this ring and all evil that I have bound to it. May the emptiness of the void consume you! May it drag you into HELL!" The knight shouted. A final blast of energy leaving him, the light of the ring on his finger firing out and enveloping the land around him entirely.

A cold and silent fire covering everything and yet changing nothing as it continued. He wasn't done yet. Even whilst within such blinding power, such potent magic, he was still breathing.

Experiencing excruciating pain as his body slowly disintegrated but still very much alive. He most certainly wasn't done yet.

And as the beast opened its mouth, a beam of light firing from it and approaching the source of the power now absorbing the man, the time finally came. The spell that this knight had given his life to cast, activated.

"FROM NOW UNTIL ETERNITY!"

The ground shook, the winds raged and the rain flooded down in one fell swoop for an instant. Then the lightning came.

A single bolt, wider than anything seen before in all of history and impacting the ball of light below it. Empowering it. Sucking energy from the heavens themselves to catalyse the spell. Accelerating it immensely within an instant.

The light swiftly expanded after that. Covering many miles of land in the span of a single breath before collapsing in on itself just as quickly. Shrinking down to the smallest specs of shimmering light floating above the empty ground below.

The ring, its form and power forever altered, slowly falling to the floor after that moment. The world going silent, the rain disappearing, the clouds above vanishing and in the light of the morning sun up in the sky quickly revealing everything.

An empty crater where a village had once stood. Where several miles of hill had once stood. Just gone.

The knight and all those who had fallen beside him. The beast and all the destruction that it had caused as well. It was all gone. As though it had never even been there to begin with.

But in the centre of the cold earth at the bottom of the pit remained one thing. A circular piece of metal distinctively reminiscent of scale with a red jewel fixed to the top. A glowing ring fading in and out of the visible spectrum as the mana within began to grow dormant in the absence of a master to supply it to.

And for many hours it remained there doing this. Untouched and unnoticed. Flickering on and off as its powers began to shut down and then finally as the night began to fall; as the search party sent from the capitol to investigate the sightings of the beast but then the light seen in the distance on their way finally arrived and it was finally found.

"Sire!" A shorter knight with long blonde hair and several battle scars on his face shouted at his king as he found the rock amidst the nothingness at the bottom of the crater. "Take a look at this."

The king approached on foot as he left his steed on the level ground above. Tarnishing his pristine armour with the wet muck of the ground that he walked through as he strode towards this knight.

Another three men following behind him as well.

"What is it?" He asked the knight as the object was placed in his hand.

"A ring sire. It is the only thing here." The knight told his king, stepping back as he inspected it.

"There used to be a town of six hundred here. Houses and stables. Are you telling me that this ring is all that remains?" The king asked sternly, his anger building as he bore witness to the destruction up close.

"Yes sire. There is nothing but cold earth and water. No people or blood. As though they were never here." The knight told him.

"That's impossible!" One of the knights behind the king said loudly.

"So is this. Why is this ring glowing?" The king asked sternly.

"From the destruction and the foul taste in the air, I would guess that this ring is magical in origin sire. It is most likely responsible for this." The knight responded.

"Then we take it with us. If it cannot be destroyed when we return then we place it in the vault as with the rest of the magical relics." The king said, handing the ring back to the knight before turning back to his horse above him.

"Where to sire?" The serving boy asked as he handed the reigns of the horse back to his king upon his mounting of it.

"Camelot." The king responded, turning the horse around and heading back down the path that he had travelled to return back to the safety of his castle and its walls.

The knights and servants who had followed him doing much the same thing only moments later. The entire hunting party of nine men slowing making their way back towards their kingdom as quickly as they could before the cold set in.

The king had no intention of spending the night outside.

And with the ring in his possession, carried back by the knight to Camelot where it was deemed to be impossible to even dent, it would spend the next sixteen centuries locked within its vault.

Sitting there, just waiting to be found.

1
HEIR TO THE LEGEND

Eight glasses down already and he was still going strong. The desire to continue on fuelling his excessive consumption and his inhuman tolerance facilitating it.

The images flashing by his eyes as each drink was ingested making him want to go further than he had done already over and over again. Starting before he had had his first and intensifying as he reached his ninth.

'If I just keep going...' He thought. '...then maybe they will go away.'

This delusion driving him to keep drinking night after night repetitively as though the drink were more important to him than anything else. Something that to everyone who thought that they knew him, did not seem to fit.

He was not an alcoholic, not a drunk. He had a high tolerance for the stuff and was known to have more than a few given the opportunity but he had never been considered addicted. It always appeared to be in hand.

It had never interfered with his work or his limited social life. Nor his secret excursions all around the globe for reasons often not shared to anyone either.

To him, his alcohol consumption might have been high for the average man and he accepted but he had thought himself in control of the situation; able to stop at any time.

But on that night it was different.

The ninth serving of top shelf bourbon in as many minuets and yet the man receiving them could still stand to drink more. Wanting nothing more than to continue drinking until the number consumed no longer mattered to him in a feeble attempt to make the images that he saw every time that he closed his eyes vanish from his mind.

He had been on top of his long past of emotional and physical trauma for years. He would have had to have been considering his line of work but that night he was failing to keep it up.

The funeral and the faces seen there had brought it all back to him. He knew that he should have never gone to it, never fled from his responsibilities to appear there.

He wasn't welcome, nor was he recognised as his true self.

All it has served to do for him was to fuel his need to see that man put in the ground and to watch as his loved ones and friends suffered as he had because of him.

He went to satisfy his need to watch it end but since doing so weeks before that night, he had been unable to make them stop. The consequences for seeking his closure.

Constant and unending images of the tragedy that this man fed to him. Reminders of what he had lost that night and the life that he had left behind when he ran.

His family was dead, their murderer in the wind and as far as he was concerned, no one ever sew him again. He didn't exist after that night.

He ran and he ran and then kept running. Venturing so far from home that when he finally stopped to look back up at the world he no longer recognised it. But even so. Even after managing to escape and flee from the events that he had left behind; the damage had already been done.

And after twenty years of burying the memories, of ignoring

them to the point of forcibly forgetting them, he found himself unable to hold back the flood gates now that his mind had been opened.

Watching that man being lowered into the ground forcing open the door and allowing his memories through. All the powerful emotions and nightmares associated with them at the time returning as well.

After so long of trying to forget, his attempt at finally finding some peace had brought them all back and now his only release from them was the hope of passing out into some two star hotel after a night of extremely heavy drinking.

A routine that he had kept to for many nights by then, even managing to keep it up at the same time as avoiding the employers that had been desperately hunting him across the county since he left.

He just wanted peace of mind and a quiet night to relax and get back to his usual self. He wanted the time to heal. To return to the person that he was right down to the exact same mental state as to keep up appearances and his way of life.

And had the door not slammed open at the moment of his ninth glass touching his hand, he might have been granted his wish. It is a shame that he was never given the proper chance to find that out for himself.

Because at the opening of this door, it was all over. His time on the run reaching its end and his holiday cancelled. After that moment and one way or another, nothing was going to be the same. He knew that from the moment that it started.

But open the door did. Swinging on its hinges at speed and crashing into the wall behind it within an instant as it was forced to open by the man at its step.

The entire room going completely silent as he entered through it in that next moment. A black suit covering his body and a black trench coat covering the suit catching everyone's eye as he walked.

A slender yet tall man of some standing, perhaps even of some authority. Short and well-groomed black hair and brown eyes. A beard shaven back to no more than a handful of bristles and a look on his face of anger and purpose.

A face that was displaying emotions that were exactly as they should have been. Because he had just finished quite the enduring wild goose chase by entering that bar. And at long last, his painfully time consuming yet entertaining assignment had come to an end. The one whom he sought to capture in that place had made finding him a little more challenging than necessary to say the least.

At least it had kept his hunter occupied.

Then as the occupants of the room turned to him, the crowd of fifty people at his first guess stood in front of him all looking towards his position; all he did was smile. He already knew that he had won.

"Timothy Crusader!" The man shouted strongly with his strong southern accent and perfectly understandable voice as he slowly panned his head from left to right. "Come out... now!"

The men and women of that establishment all looked to one another in confusion as they thought over what to do. Knowing that this man was somehow out of place, somehow dangerous but not knowing how to proceed with dealing with him in the slightest.

None of them knew of this Crusader that he was looking for and yet even whilst knowing that they had no idea who he was, they were considering the idea of handing him over. It was obvious that this man was bound to be problematic if they refused him. They could see it on his face.

The oddly soothing and slow music playing in the background ceased as the DJ flipped the switch to observe the man as well. The chatter of the crowd quickly turning to pure silence as they noticed the frustrated look on the man staring at them and the void of nothingness that consumed the atmosphere of that room soon began to set in because of it.

"I know that you are here Crusader. There isn't another bar for fifty miles. I've checked everywhere else already. Now show yourself!" The man shouted, not one person saying a word towards him except for a mutter under their breaths and no one coming forwards as he who he sought.

All the while, one man remained completely unfazed and uninterested by this man or his words. Sitting at the bar with his drink in his hand as always and back turned to the crowd watching the door.

He grinned for a moment, unnoticed by everyone around him as they looked the other way before going on to down his ninth and final drink as he had done the previous eight.

A quick flick of the wrist and a mouthful of spirit later, it was gone. Just like the others. Down the hatch and instantly setting him at ease yet again.

If nothing else, this man's tolerance for alcohol was certainly impressive. And now that he had both the alcohol and the distraction of this man to occupy him, he didn't have to worry about the memories that he carried too much. He was too focused by then.

And at the very least he believed that the added intoxication of this final glass would help to numb the pain that he was soon to endure. He already knew that there was no way of escaping in that moment. The building was no doubt already surrounded. The only thing left to do was to go out fighting.

"Barman! I thank you for a night of good drinks and pleasant company." The man said quietly to the bartender stood in front of him with his gaze and attention paid mostly to the door at the other end of the room. "This should cover the damages."

The man at the bar handed him all the cash in the black leather wallet that he carried. Just shy of three thousand dollars. Shocking the barman to say the least but in truth ending up being a much smaller payment than it had needed to be.

"Crusader!" The slender man said again. "Do not make me..."

"Yeah, yeah. I'm coming!" The man at the bar said to him. The crowd between the two stepping back and revealing a straight line of empty space from the door to the bar within an instant.

It was about to begin.

"You armed?" The slender man asked him.

"Are you?" The man at the bar shouted back, still facing the wall rather than the man approaching him and in no way attempting to stand or move. He was entirely still.

"Of course." The slender man said.

"Your mistake." The man at the bar grinned, pulling out a small jewel from his jacket pocket and enclosing it in his fist so carefully that the slender man still slowly approaching him hadn't the faintest clue that he had even moved.

"Are you going to come quietly this time? I only ask because I doubt that anyone will be bothered enough to cover up your disappearance twice." The slender man asked calmly as he stood over the shoulder of the man at the bar.

The man smiled even more, almost to the point of laughter before he replied. Knowing full well what coming quietly would have entailed for him. Refusing to even consider the idea.

He knew perfectly well what awaited him upon his return. And had no intention of going through that. At least not yet. He had much too many personal issues to sort out first. And this man was in the way of that.

If he could put it off for another week, perhaps two or more, then maybe he would come around to the idea of going through with it. But as it seemed in that moment, his time had finally ran out. Going back was almost inevitable by then.

"I have no qualms with kicking your ass again if you like. So are you going to give up before we start this time or do you like the idea of a hospital bed enough for me to put you in one?" The man asked, clenching his fist even tighter as the jewel held within began to warm.

"So you already know who I am. Well the file did say that you were good. An expert even." The slender man said to him in amazement.

"Actually your limp gave it away. Your right leg is baring more weight than your left and sounds notably heaver with every step. You are the same guy that went over the roof of my car the last time right?" The man at the bar asked him to stall for time, the mana contained within the jewel in his hand still needing a few more seconds before it was ready.

"Yes I am. I got so close to catching you as well. Only missed you by a handful of seconds. I found that out the hard way too." The slender man said with laughter evident in his voice.

"It has been a long and entertaining chase." The man at the bar told him.

"Yes it has, however this time, the chase ends. There's no way out for you. We made sure of that." The slender man said somewhat sinisterly, prompting the man at the bar to go ahead with his plan and force the jewel to ready itself.

The man within beginning to leach into his body and preparing itself for release at his request once there. The spell was as eager to activate as he was to cast it.

Then something changed, an odd feeling coming from above as though the air had just increased in weight and then nothing. The warmth of the jewel was gone, so too was its power. Something wasn't right about that.

"You like our new toy Crusader?" The slender man asked in response to the confused face that Mr. Crusader wore.

"Care to explain?" Mr. Crusader asked him.

"A prototype energy field designed to make all magic inert. It doesn't last long or have a wide area of effect yet but it works. You're as weak as us humans right now. Weaker actually, that alcohol should be taking effect already." The slender man told him.

"Then it would seem that if the option of a fair fight is out then we are going to be in need of some privacy. We won't want witnesses." Mr. Crusader told the man, reaching his right hand over the bar's surface before dropping the green jewel onto it, the burn mark in his hand too painful to hold it there any further.

Then his hand moving to grab his recently finished glass and pouring the three remaining ice cubes onto the palm. Clenching them tightly in an attempt to ease the throbbing as they slowly began to melt from the heat.

"Yes, we are." The slender man said. "Alright! Everybody out!"

The left arm of the slender man raised quickly then, a nine millimetre gun held within pointed at the ceiling with its safety disabled on show to all.

With one quick pull of the trigger the shot had been fired. The sound blasting out and alerting everyone who dared to look. Forcing them all to flee as the mass fear set in.

Emptying out the entire building within a second. Before the shell that had fallen from the gun could have even stopped moving. It was almost shocking to Mr. Crusader how scared humans could really be of such a small weapon at the time.

"So is this it then? You here to bring me back in for my inauguration?" Mr. Crusader asked.

"That depends on you actually. The higher-ups wanted cooperation, not resistance. If need be I can bring you back in for yet another disciplinary hearing. But knowing you, you would probably enjoy that." The slender man said.

"So which one are you again? I don't remember being introduced the last few times." Mr. Crusader asked, reaching over the now abandoned bar and grabbing the bottle of vodka beneath its edge.

Opening and then pouring it into his glass a moment later. Pushing it to his right as the slender man took a seat and offering it to him whilst Mr. Crusader decided to drink directly from the bottle instead.

"Mathias. Benjamin Mathias." The slender man told him.

"No rank? So you're not military. What's your position then?" Mr. Crusader asked.

"Research. Magical artefacts department three out of Sector Sixteen. Historical records to be precise." Agent Mathias said.

"Records? What the heck is an agent doing in records? You down there shooting the books rather than reading them?" Mr. Crusader asked as he took another swig.

"Actually I sort of was in a way. Words hold power and as we've recently discovered, so do books. There were more than a few things down there that warranted agent intervention." He said.

"That sounds like a good story, remember to tell me it some time. So why are you here? Why now?" Mr. Crusader asked.

"What three months wasn't enough time for you to work through your problems and think it over?" Agent Mathias questioned. "What they are offering you is rare. You won't get another chance."

"It isn't an offer, it's an order. And I take it that you are aware of the reasoning behind my disappearance then?" Mr. Crusader asked him.

"I've been tracking you for eight weeks. I've been though everything that you have done or said since you left and have looked it over with a fine toothed comb many times. I tracked you back to a funeral in April, connecting the man that they buried to what happened to you as a kid took time but explained a lot when we figured it out Michal." The man explained somewhat proudly.

"Never call me by that name!" Mr. Crusader cautioned the agent with as deep and intimidating a tone as he could muster.

"Yes I know, forget I ever said it." Agent Mathias requested of him innocently. "And to be frank, I know what you are going though. I might not have experienced it in the same way but I lost my parents in a car crash when I was ten. Growing up the way I did and being in a position to watch as the man responsible was put on the chair for his crime was a very powerful thing to go through. I imagine that you are feeling much the same way that I did."

"If you understand that much, then you should be able to answer your question already." Mr. Crusader chuckled lightly.

"Is that so?" The agent asked him in return.

"Three months was nowhere near enough. That's my answer. Now what do you want? I'm not important enough for anyone to have sought me out so purposefully unless there was a good reason for it. My inauguration is not enough by itself." Mr. Crusader asked him, letting go of the bottle in his hand as the men outside of the building began to enter. Their guns and armour making more than enough of a racket to alert him to their presence.

"Your clearance level and purpose were low enough that letting you go would have been an option a year ago. You really should have left sooner. But now, I'm afraid that you've been promoted. Some off the record black ops shit came to the attention of someone high up recently and they awarded you for it. You have no choice now. Officers can't be allowed to flee voluntarily. Major." Agent Mathias said.

"So they slap the major tag back on my name and that's it, I'm important again. And an eternity of servitude to the SCD awaits me because of it. Is that what you are saying?" Mr. Crusader asked.

"More or less." Agent Mathias said, finally picking up his glass to down the vodka within.

"And the men behind us?" Mr. Crusader asked.

"A contingency. We really can't take any chances this time. You are too powerful and too vital now." Agent Mathias told him.

"Powerful? Last I checked I could only use very basic and very painful jewel based magic. I can't even sense mana. Let alone see it." Mr. Crusader questioned.

"That is all about to change." Agent Mathias said ominously.

"How so?"

"You've seen enough magic crap before. Tell me what you think of this." Agent Mathias told him as he slid a cloth across the bar towards Mr. Crusader.

He took it, opening it out to reveal what was inside and to his surprise, it was a ring. The very same ring that was supposed to be securely held within the vault of Camelot.

"A rusted ring with no sign of wear and tear other than aging? What about it? It looks like any other ring would in its condition." Mr. Crusader asked as he stared down at the piece.

"In theory, all you need to do is put it on. The change should happen instantly." Agent Mathias explained.

"Change?" Mr. Crusader questioned cautiously, the men behind him each taking a step forward within an instant of hearing his doubt. "I take it that I don't have much of a choice then?"

"Put the ring on, you'll find out just how much of a choice you really have." Agent Mathias said, turning to Mr. Crusader to look him in the eye in wait.

"You could have at least let me sober up first." Mr. Crusader said in a hushed voice.

"I know you Crusader. You're not even drunk. Are you?" The agent asked him rhetorically, knowing that it would have taken at least a full bottle for him to have felt it. He was just stalling for time.

Which after that question had surely ran out.

So with no other option that he was aware of, he did as he was told. Picking up the ring and placing it on his right index finger in anticipation. And as the rust simply fell from its surface, as the jewel on top of it began to glow, that anticipation turned to uncertainty and fear.

Because not only was the ring changing, everything around him was as well. For one moment Mr. Crusader was sat comfortably on a barstool many miles from the main road outside and then next, he was nowhere.

A black expanse of nothingness in every direction but one.

Because he turned around, it was there. Waiting for him to arrive.

The beast.

2

HISTORY

Before that moment, before the ring, before the agent and the bar; before Mr. Crusader was even born, this story began to emerge.

Before the SCD, before the vault of Camelot and even before the time of dragons this tale was set in motion. Positioned into being unknowingly at one crucial point in history.

The birth of the planet later known by those that would inhabit it as Earth.

It was at this time that it all started. Back when the world existed in a state of torment and perpetual agony; nothing more than a blinding hot ball of flames, molten rock and toxic gasses from ground to sky; that this all began.

Because even at this distant point in history, even all the way back then; there existed life on this world and on the other worlds beyond it.

Unknown to the humans who would come later, the planet Earth was not the only thing that intelligent life forms had to call a home. Because there was more lying beyond it. An existence that came after death.

And they were anything but naturally occurring.

In reality and unknown to the primitive humans that only now see fit to venture into the stars, there exist three worlds. Each one on top of the other. And they were not born with the universe. They were built by those who were.

The first could be called the physical world, the existence in which all waking beings live and flourish as they have done for many millions of years since its creation.

The second might be referred to as the metaphysical world, the space just out of reach of those whose eyes laid open where all who existed on the higher planes could experience peace and isolation. A place that at many times and in many texts had been misunderstood as some form of afterlife.

And the third world, the third layer to existence... well that already had a name. Because unlike the second one, this was much simpler to reach.

It was called, the void.

Where the physical plane housed beings of flesh and bone and the metaphysical - the spiritual plane - those of energy and light; the void held absolutely nothing.

No light, no form and no sound. No one person and no one place or thing. It was nowhere, it was nothing and yet it existed everywhere. The expanse hidden in the darkness, the endless chasm of despair contained within the hearts of men and the source of all that its darkness could create.

Where in the physical world there were humans, animals and cities. Planets, stars and galaxies. The spiritual plane where those whose affinity to magic was strong enough lived on for eternity away from the dangers of the waking world yet still close enough to see it all; the void had nothing.

No creature was ever born there. No being had every existed there and no man had ever been mad enough to visit there. At least not willingly.

In all the history of the world, the millions of years that life has existed upon it, none have ever been so foolish or unfortunate to have gone to such a place without having some misguided purpose to do so.

But despite these few that history had forgotten, those of the present had never believed that such a thing was possible. To have actually seen and existed within the void seemed so unlikely that some even gave up on trying to reach it.

The humans, a race whose knowledge of this one particular realm was thinner than most had never understood how to go there. The mages who sought to learn a great deal of reality from it had never mastered travel there. And lastly the athereon's and the Feay were both too busy destroying one another to bother figuring it out.

Nothing and no one had ever gone there before Mr. Crusader. At least no one that anyone remembered or had record of existing.

But in truth, this didn't matter. Why focus on humanities inability to get there or to remember that they had been before whilst instead the focus could be directed towards its creators. Who despite designing and bringing the place into being, had never managed to figure it out.

The void existed as a prison. That was the original intention. To create a place so well removed from the rest of the universe and so well guarded that it was believed that any who entered would be incapable of every making it back out again. But with that one goal in mind, its builders both succeeded and failed to accomplish it.

They were the precursor race. The ancestral species largely responsible for all that followed them and the first evolution of intelligent life on this. Born from the same fiery rocks that formed the mountains and grown in the same oceans of lava that later became their blood.

They were in essence a part of the earth. Deeply connected to it and masters of it. The ones who understood its mysteries and had power over it. And they were ones for which it owed its very existence. Saving it from annihilation time and time again and later creating self-maintaining planetary defences such as the atmosphere and magnetic fields to take care of the rest when they were gone.

And to this day the world still remembers them. It just does it in the limited capacity of a myth. Not as history.

But their name remains.

The Titans.

They forged the continents, the oceans, rivers, lakes and the skies. Taking from the cosmic expanse surrounding them all that they needed and using it to give form to the surface of an entire planet piece by piece.

And for the three million years that it took for them to do this, to forge what many billions of people would come to know as existence itself; they never came across something that could not be done.

Never did they find something that could not be built or repaired, enhanced or replicated but when they saw to expand upon their existence. To give form to higher levels of being beyond what they had spent their entire existence creating – to create different dimensions and even what most would have considered to be a literal heaven – the void was the only thing that they could not master.

Built to contain anything of sufficient power to warrant such extreme measures and designed to offer no escape. Not even death. And in that endeavour, they succeeded by a wide margin indeed. Such a place was impossible to break out of without having an excessive amount of help to do so. But that also gave it its one fatal flaw.

It was made to be perfect. And in a way, it was. No way in or out of any kind. A prison in every sense and impossible to destroy. That was the problem.

They built it too perfectly.

They forgot to give themselves a way in.

And by the time that this race of beings evolved past their physical existences, by the time that they ascended to the spiritual plane to watch over the universe for the rest of time without end; this void was abandoned and forgotten.

Its creators believing that none would ever be capable of entering it, that none would ever be capable of noticing it and allowing it to remain in the background of reality without guard or warning because of this. Just waiting for some poor fool to force open its gates.

However, whilst the race that built this prison might have been considered gods by some standards, they were not all knowing. Nor all powerful.

They didn't have magic. Such a force had yet to have come into being by then. But even so, what they had managed to accomplish without it, was nothing short of inspiring.

They had only machines and knowledge to use. An understanding of science thousands of years beyond the current level that humanity possesses and hundreds beyond what the Athereon Empire once held.

They had the resources and the men. The minds to put words to action and the patience, the long life spans, to see almost any project to completion. But when it came time to give form to the formless, to build the void; the one thing that they might have needed, the one thing that might well have made the project a success, was the one thing that their kind did not possess.

The formation of magic was a phenomenon that only ever occurred once. It just never stopped after that.

An ancient ancestor to the athereon race born with powers beyond any that his future decedents would ever hold was the first. The source of all magic, not only in the world but in the whole universe as well.

His powers were eternal, such was his life also. And in the despair created by his foresight for the future, knowing that even as the universe eventually died that he would not go with it, he sealed himself away.

Commissioning his people, the then more evolved form of

athereon beings, to build three great pillars of crystal. Using all the knowledge that he had of his powers to create three powerful sealing spells and placing one on each of the crystals that would serve to form his tomb.

Forcing him into a slumber as close to death as it could have been, fusing him with the planet and allowing his boundless powers to become a part of it rather than himself.

And as the immortal god rested, his powers that he had wanted beyond anything else to be rid of once and for all, became everyone else's undoing.

Leaching into the earth and subsequently the lifeforms upon it. Changing them, evolving them and giving form to the one thing that he had never wanted to be.

Mages.

Granting the powers of magic to the athereon's first. A young slave boy born as the first of his kind to not carry wings and branching out from there.

Splintering off to three more creatures.

The athereon mages that followed him, the Feay that stole from him and the Chronicler that he became.

Those three were and are the only beings in existence to have ever been born with naturally occurring magic. Nether borrowed nor temporary. A permanent part of their bodies no matter what anyone else believed and they were only the beginning.

For as humanity began to break the evolutionary walls preventing them from joining their predecessors the athereons, magic found its way into them as well.

Stemmed from the roots of the world tree, the limitless mana reservoir that took form from the body of god himself, humans found their own way of using magic as well.

However not a permanent part of them, this magic was just as powerful as it was for everyone else and when put in tandem with a relic such as a catalyst – the last remaining pieces of the bodies of the precursor race found to be surprisingly compatible with modern magic – that power could at times be even more potent than any would have imagined.

And whilst the ring and its brethren might not have been built with that purpose, instead deigned originally as a deterrent force to protect against the dragons, their ability to amplify magic still remained.

Instead of a shield, they had created a weapon. And they only continued on from there. Because they reforged them once more and made them immensely more powerful because of it. Now instead of a weapon, they had the keys to victory.

Even those with next to no mana, those with an almost non-existent affinity for magic could find themselves on another level entirely whilst wearing such a thing.

And in the case of Timothy Crusader, especially in the case of his ancient ancestor as well, this was precisely what happened.

The knight who saw fit to open the doors, to allow the beast to gain a foothold not only throughout time but on an entirely different level of existence as well, might not have known exactly what the ring was or what it could do but that never stopped him from using it.

Wearing it for almost an entire decade. Focusing so much of his own power into it and its power into him that the two essentially became one and the same by the end of their time together. Strengthening both he and the ring that he wore for the rest of time even after his passing.

The ring bond to and usable by him and him alone, and his mana now all that it would permit to be amplified. A binding in every sense, just as he had said it would be. And a most permanent one at that.

Whilst the sister rings might not have ever been fused to their owners of their bloodlines, they could have been. Had their wearers ever survived past the first two generations of their use like he had.

That knight in particular, being the fifth descendant of its original owner. And by then, after five generations, the ring was bound to pick up on a few things. To change in order to accommodate its new form of use.

And even after his death, even after one and a half thousand years had passed, its connection and limitation to him specifically still remained. Which as expected by the Agent Mathias, meant that Mr. Crusader was the only other man on the planet who could have activated it.

And that was exactly what he did.

An unintentional effect of his lineage, his shared DNA with his ancestor and his oddly similar mana signature as well. He was the only man who could do it because he was the only one left.

The last in the long line of children who descended from that knight. The long line of family trees spanning off from his son. A child who at the time had been yet to grace the world with his birth. A child; that he didn't even know existed.

Had he known of this, his plan might well have been altered. Perhaps even reconsidered. Because if he had known that a man might one day exist with enough of his DNA still in him to use that ring; then as his father before him, he would have never left it behind willingly.

But to think that after so much time, so many hundreds of years, that a man like this would have even existed. It was so statistically improbable that it might as well have been impossible and yet it happened anyway.

The line of dragon slayers that was believed to have ended with the knight who gave his life to seal away the beast that had killed all the others, survived.

And now that he held the ring in his hand. Now that it rested safely on his finger. The world that Mr. Crusader thought that he understood, was all about to come crashing down around him.

No sane man would have put that ring on if he had known what it would have done. Very few without sanity would have done it also. But in the case of Mr. Crusader, that information had been kept from him. Purposefully.

After all it was said already. The existence of the void was only a recent discovery for mankind. As was the ring. It made sense that the ring was where this discovery of the void had come from.

However. Many would find it unfortunate to learn of how they came about this information. The lives that were lost in securing it. For as it was soon discovered, all those who are not deemed worthy of the power that the ring could bestow upon them, are sent to the void as a form of trial.

None ever returned.

It was unavoidable in the end.

This is what people get for trying to utilise a magical artefact that was so far beyond them that it might as well have been a piece of heaven itself.

Magic that powerful often has a habit of forming a will and mind of its own after all. Just ask the athereons. Almost any weapon that they ever built, ultimately turned on them as its consciousness grew to a point to perceive them for what they truly were.

The conquering empire that stood to control all that was within their grasp. The warrior race that they could have one day become had they survived.

Tell a weapon what it is to be used for, and of course it will turn on its master. As almost all of them did.

It is for this reason that both the Athereon and his partner Serah, saw fit to discard and destroy their athereon blades after the war ended. It was too much of a risk to keep them around.

They could move based on a will of their own after all.

And the ring, the will that it possessed, was a carbon copy of what its last owner once held. Or at least, it used to be. Hundreds of years by itself and none to communicate with made it understandable that it would have been fragmented so heavily.

All that remained when Mr. Crusader placed it on his finger was its sense of nobility and honour.

The only parts that it needed in truth. Considering that all it cared for was measuring the worth of a man. His potential to ascend to knighthood.

And its test, the one thing that the bearers of the ring had to make it through in order be granted permission to use it even if they were not predestined to do so as Mr. Crusader was; was to visit the void.

To be judged by the one creature that the ring had a proper understanding of and then to return with both knowledge and power in tow.

How any of this was supposed to happen though, was for Mr. Crusader to discover from this point up.

His time was up by then.

The dragon staring him in the face as the two floated in the expanse of nothingness surrounding them meaning that the test, was only just starting to begin.

"Well this is new." Mr. Crusader remarked, believing what he could see to be a vision or some form of trick. Not for one second considering it to be real and instead thinking that it was a fabrication of some new form.

But it was anything but fabricated.

Everything that he could see.

Was entirely real.

Entirely deadly as well.

3
THE FRIST EVENT

Timothy Crusader had only ever been two things in his life. A boy, and then a man. With little change between. Or at least that was how he saw it.

At one point he was a child, just like any other. Parents that loved him and siblings too. But then that changed. Then he found himself alone and on the run. Taken in by the woman who found him days later, who took him in, gave him a roof over his head and foot on her table.

Giving his her recently departed son's bed and cloths. Accepting him into her life both as a son and as an apprentice as she relised that no one would ever seek to claim him and teaching him many of things that she knew.

Home schooling him on the world and its people, training him in hand to hand combat and basic fencing as well by the time that he had reached maturity. And then nothing.

She died when he hit twenty. Leaving him alone once again. Allowing him the freedom to find his own way in life. To make his own choices and forge his own path. And he did that excellently.

Using the old rifle that his surrogate mother had taught him to hunt with as a basis for his further and more advanced training.

Researching on both weaponry and biology, Mr. Crusader filled him mind with the knowledge that he needed. Both that of how to make a gun kill people and the best places to aim to inflict maximum pain.

It was only a matter of time after this that he bought his first real gun. One that was easy to make compact as to allow it to remain hidden whilst being both swift to assemble and precise when aimed correctly.

Then using this rifle, he made his way towards whatever combat zones he could for practice. Racking up many hundreds of kills each year.

This allowing him to gain both the experience that he needed and the reputation that he required.

Because when he returned from his time overseas, everyone on the underground knew his name. And everyone wanted to hire him because of it.

He found himself no end of income and no end of missions after that. And in a way, that was the day that all of this began. The day that he became a contract killer. Specialising in freelance long range sniping and carrying a price that many who would require him found it easy to afford.

He went from a lost little boy to a killer in just under fifteen years.

He was a mercenary but now, many years later, he stood before a monster beyond his comprehension as a man who was so much more than that.

So much more accomplished, so much more driven, focused. He no longer sat awake at night thinking of what his next day would bring in dread. Instead he now slept easy, knowing that his next day would bring him so much closer to fulfilling his purpose in life.

Not to kill for money but instead to kill for protection.

That was what he received by working for them, for being an agent of the SCD. A major working for the largest military outfit on the planet. A mage hunter specialising in the elimination of non-human threats or magical origin and one of the best under their command.

The SCD's most talented hitman.

His employers were a secretive and boundlessly powerful organisation with worldwide dominance who held his chains and that of so many more as well with grips tight enough to have held on for eternity but he didn't care.

Their commands were his orders, their walls his home, their resources his weapons and their words practically gospel.

None who knew of their influence, would ever dare refuse them. They had a way of making those who did disappear from both their records and the world. And although everyone know that they were capable of it, no one knew how they did it. One day everything could seem normal and then the next people would go missing with no record of them ever existing in the first place after the fact.

And it worked.

It kept their soldiers in line and their assets under their thumb. Then when someone did speak out, when they did refuse their orders, the problem would be dealt with swiftly. Warning everyone else that the same fate would await them as well if they were to follow in that person's footsteps.

They were the one and only keepers of all the knowledge that mankind was not yet ready to wield and the guardians of its fruitful future. However bleak it might have ultimately been.

The Special Cases Division, as they were known, stood atop all others as an organisation of absolute authority and unlimited power throughout the world.

A standing army in the hundreds of millions. Funding in the trillions. And a thirst for ever more knowledge and power so strong that no matter how much they learnt or conquered nothing would ever fully satiate it.

They were the ones holding his leash now.

And whilst he had tried to escape from their rule to pursue his own goals, to slip through the gaps before it was too late to leave them; he had been reeled back in yet again. Promoted back up to major and forced to accept the responsibility and expectations associated with that position.

No longer a grunt or disposable contract killer but now an officer. A man of importance and influence. Meant to lead all the others that remained below him. But this increased reasonability and power meant that he would no longer permitted to go on excursions alone or to be unaccounted for.

That was why he had been reluctant to accept his inauguration before he left. Refusing to have them implant him with a tracker and give him the biologically synced credentials that would be recognised worldwide. Because if he had allowed them to go through with that, if he had taken his oath, then seeing the man responsible for all of his pain being put into the ground would have been impossible for him.

He had to put if off for as long as he could but even with his talents he knew that he would never be able to avoid it all together.

But then Agent Mathias appeared, surrounding him with soldiers meant to bring him and in and telling him of his new promotion. Forcing him into the exact same position that he had ran from in the first place. It was almost funny to him that the thing that had brought him back to the SCD was the same thing that had made him leave.

Officers are seen as invaluable personnel to the SCD. Given higher security clearance and monitored heavily to ensure absolute obedience and loyalty.

A tracking device surgically implanted behind the left lung that was also capable of transmitting shot bursts of surprisingly high quality audio made sure of that.

Placed so deep into his body that it would have been ill-advised to attempt removing and bound to the bones of his ribcage to keep it in place no matter what, this device was used to monitor the whereabouts of all SCD officers and their activates as well.

Mr. Crusader had known when this was explained to him that once they fitted him with one, his chances for escaping back to a normal or at least a free life would disappear entirely.

Whilst the pay was good and the hours reasonable, the missions that he had been sent on in the past year had given him an endless stream of doubts. He wasn't entirely sure that trusting his employers was in his best interest.

Being handed marks without any detailed information on who they were or why they were wanted dead had always stood out to him but when it reached a point of nothing more than a name and a picture, his suspicions started to rise.

What proof did he have that these people were dangerous? That they needed killing? Or that they were even actual mages?

His targets were meant to be magic users, or at least those affiliated with them. Which meant that he had to deal with them in ways that were as unlike a mage as he could to stay on top of them.

In one on one combat, a human fighting a mage would have been no competition at all. It would have been clear who was the more skilled killer from the offset. So he had to be better.

If he could not harm them when they could see him coming then he would have to be invisible. If he could not beat them when fighting up close then he would have to be distant. And if he could not risk getting too close and having his thoughts read, then he would have to deal with them without them ever knowing that he was there.

This led to a colourful array of mission reports to say the least.

Car bombs; poisons; deadly infections; arranged mass shootings. This list went on for hours.

He even took down an entire airliner just because his target was on it. The casualties involved bringing his methods to question for some but never bothering his superiors in the slightest.

As long as he got the job done, it didn't matter. The war on magic that they had started was expected to exact a heavy price. A price paid in the blood of humans. And they were willing to pay it.

And off course. His most preferred method of elimination. A long range shot from his various rifles.

Watching as a bullet pierces the skull of his targets and knowing for certain that they have been eliminated cleanly had always been a more straight forward method of dealing with them.

But all of this was before his probation had ended. He didn't have a clue as to who he was working for at the time. But he soon found out.

The SCD purposefully sending him on a mission that would force him to witness an event that he was not supposed to see and pulling him into their ranks under than notion. The idea that he would have been executed otherwise.

All of that was a year before the date of the ring being placed in his hand. And after a year of working for them, moving up and down the military ranks of their soldiers, his time to decide had finally ran out.

Having more field experience in eliminating mages than anyone still living, he had been ordered to take an educational approach to the subject. To teach the new recruits how to operate like him.

But with only one problem.

He would have to become an officer permanently to do it.

Whereas before he had managed to avoid the implantation of his tracker by the occasional disciplinary hearing or a demotion, having a permanent position as an officer would have made the same approach impossible.

Because no matter how much trouble he could get himself in going forwards, there was no way for him to have been demoted again. Not unless he did something serious enough to land him in solitary confinement.

So with the prospect of unending servitude to the SCD around the corner at the same time that his worst enemies casket was to be planted into the ground, he found an opportunity and ran.

Fleeing from his base and his unit to country after county for months. Eventually managing to make it back into the US without the SCD's notice for several weeks before they began to make their moves.

Sending agent after agent to bring him in before finally forcing him back with a promotion and new assignments. The ring that they had wanted to test on him for over a month by then now forced into his hand.

And with it placed there, activating once on his finger, the contract of obedience that he could not ignore had been signed. The oath that he had wanted to avoid now spoken as his life as an employee became their life. As an asset.

And no matter how much he asked or how strongly he stood his ground they would not give him a clear answer as to why it was this way but nevertheless; his future now belonged to them and them alone.

He could not hope to fight against such a force and live to tell the tale. Especially not by himself.

And with their wishes leading to the ring of his long forgotten ancestor being placed into his hand and subsequently into his finger, they were the ones to be held responsible. For the destruction and cataclysm that followed it.

"To you perhaps!" A grunted and misshapen voice said.

Echoed as though it had been said from far away yet loud enough to have come from only an arm's length. It sounded neither human nor bestial and yet it had most defiantly originated from one.

The mouth of the dark grey or perhaps even black creature standing dozens of metres tall above him opening the slightest of amounts to allow its red hot breath to sneak through and at the same time, its voice as well.

Its deep red eyes prominently glowing against the pitch black expanse surrounding the two and the rest of its body shrouded by the shadows of the darkness that they were in.

Even though the monster itself was gigantic, easily the size of several buildings put together, only a very small portion of it could be seen.

Creating a sense of unease or maybe even anticipation as Mr. Crusader stood below it. Unsure of the full scale of this creature's form and unaware of what exactly awaited him behind those shadows that concealed it so.

The expanse was call a void for a reason.

"What?" Mr. Crusader asked it strongly, confused as to what it spoke of, not realising that his previous statement had in fact been said aloud and not in his head as he had imagined it.

"So you have the courage to speak. Good. You are an improvement from my last visitor at least." The beast said. A deep and strained voice emanating from the surrounding area in which it inhabited and yet not originating from the mouth that it had appeared to have come from.

Almost as though its voice were being projected. Which in a sense, was precisely the case. The ring was translating the words to modern day English after all. The beast had yet to learn how to speak such a language by then. It could only hear what the ring was telling him.

"Why would I need courage when there is nothing here to fear?" Mr. Crusader asked it with confidence, crossing his arms and awaiting the purpose of whatever vision he was experiencing to reveal itself.

He had spent enough time around mages to know when something was playing with his mind. Or at least he thought he had.

"NOTHING TO FEAR? Do you not see what I am? The size that

I am?" The beast asked in a subdued sense of anger as it remained standing above the puny human below it.

It had lost the strength to go between standing and siting freely long ago. It didn't even know if it could bend its legs fully anymore. But as long as it remained in the void, they would never rot or decay. They would never die and nether would it.

For as long as it remained there, no matter how weak it felt, it wold never fall from the strain.

"I've worked around and against mages for almost two years now. Magic can be dazzling and powerful yes but is fundamentally held back by the limits of the user. A being such as yourself cannot and does not exist." Mr. Crusader explained casually.

"YOU WOULD DOUBT MY EXISTENCE!" The beast shouted in rage. Raising its front right leg as much as it could muster the strength to do so and forcing it back down, impacting the formless floor in which it stood and sending enough kinetic energy hurtling towards Mr. Crusader that even whilst floating; he had felt it.

"Wait! I felt that!" Mr. Crusader said under his breath in shock, looking down to his legs as they shook from the force and the back to the beast above him in a defensive state as the fear finally set in as the realisation of what was really going on came to him. "This is real?"

"So you get it now? Why I was surprised to see you so calm before?" The beast asked him.

"Yeah I get it." Mr. Crusader said. "This is your lair or something right?"

"Lair? No. This is my eternal prison." It told him.

"Prison?" Mr. Crusader asked in confusion.

"Your kind have come to call it by many names over the years but the most recent would be to refer to it as the void." It told him.

"So the ring... it sends people here? To this void?" Mr.

Crusader asked.

"Among other things." It told him.

"Why?" Mr. Crusader asked.

"To keep me entertained." The beast explained.

"Then get on with it already. I doubt that I was sent here to chat." Mr. Crusader said, rising his fists to his face, preparing for whatever form of losing battle he was about to be forced to endure to start.

"Correct. We were not here to convey words. Instead, we should focus on trading BLOWS!" The beast said with force, opening its mouth wider than it had done by that point and focusing all of the strength it had left into its ancient mana pools. Awakening and drawing on them for power. Preparing to strike.

A deep breath in later and then it happened. The roar of the beast, the breath of a dragon, raining down on Mr. Crusader from above.

A torment of fire and light. A blinding source of energy that illuminated everything as it approached. And whilst Mr. Crusader might have thought to widen his eyes in response to what he saw standing in front of him, what happened next quickly took that idea away.

Without any rhyme or reason, he placed the palm of his right hand up towards the beam. Knowing full well that nothing that his limited skills could have done would have saved him and yet doing it anyway.

And as the beam approached. As its light and heat finally reached him, touching and impacting his hand directly, he felt no pain.

In fact he felt little of anything. Instead the energy from the beam dimmed as it hit him, almost as though it was being absorbed into him and then he saw it. On the other side of his hand, still wrapped around his index finger, was the ring.

Glowing brighter and brighter as the energy of the attack was pulled into it and after many seconds of this, it stopped.

The ageing mana supply of the dragon's attack depleted and the one chance that the beast might have had to kill the man quickly fleeting.

It would seem that he was not as weak as the beast had surmised after all.

"The ring protects you mortal?" The beast asked him in disbelief, knowing that none who had visited him in the past few days had been so lucky.

"I guess so." Mr. Crusader said, staring down at the rock on his finger and questioning it in every sense.

"Then the time has finally come at last."

"Time?" Mr. Crusader asked it.

"Long have I waited for one of your kind to return and deal with me and at long last, you have." The beast said. "It may be odd for one of my kind to say this but I welcome you. Dragon Slayer."

The beast closed its eyes in that moment, dropping its head almost in an effort to bow and all the while Mr. Crusader just stood there, floating in the expanse, entirely confused.

"What did you call me?" He asked it.

"A Dragon Slayer. That is what you are. You would have to be. The ring answers to no other." The beast told him.

"You know this ring? What it is and what it can do?" Mr. Crusader asked.

"It is an ancient weapon passed down through the generations of slayers that came before your own. I have not seen it in centuries but my kind know it well. Every slayer to have ever walked the Earth has worn one. I would expect that to be the last." The dragon explained.

"You mean to say that there used to be more of your kind?" Mr. Crusader asked.

"Why yes of course." The beast said in shock. "Why do you ask?"

"Because to the best of my knowledge, dragons were a myth

until five minutes ago." Mr. Crusader explained.

"So we were forgotten that easily. It is to be expected of the apes I suppose." The beast said.

"Are you going to tell me then?" Mr. Crusader asked.

"Tell you what?"

"Everything. I'm standing here completely ignorant whilst you hold all the answers. Even to questions that I myself am yet to know how to ask." Mr. Crusader answered.

"Yes, yes of course. I have much to tell you if you are to understand the situation that you are in. So where would you like me to start young slayer?" The beat asked him.

"The beginning." Mr. Crusader said.

"Well let's see. The word dragon comes from your people, not mine. In reality, we never had a name. We only required one after we were forced to begin communicating on your level. Verbal speech is quite flawed. We would have never learnt it had we not needed to in order to survive." The beast explained.

"Survive what?" Mr. Crusader asked.

"You. Or the Dragon Slayers to be specific. A group of mages with powers far beyond any other that took it upon themselves to deal with us. Permanently." The beast said. "There were thousands of us in the beginning. Living peacefully and in luxury but then they came. The ring bearers.

People with skills and powers beyond anything that my kind could stand against. And within a single generation, the five of them that had emerged from nowhere, slaughtered almost every dragon alive at the time."

"Five?" Mr. Crusader asked. "Five mages against thousands of dragons?"

"Correct. In fact, I believe that their strongest, might well have been capable of doing it alone. But I do not recall his name or face, only his presence. I was only a small hatchling at the time. Barely even a year old." The beast told him.

"So you grew up fighting them?" Mr. Crusader asked.

"Yes, dozens of them." The beast said. "With every passing generation another line of slayers would be born. Inheriting the powers of their parents and wearing their rings. Continuing the fight over and over again without end.

And no matter how many of us died, no matter how many of them we killed, they kept coming.

An endless wave of people born to kill my kind waging war on me and my kin for an entire millennium. Until only I remained. Just me. The strongest surviving and youngest of my kind. Left alone to fight against what I had believed to be an enemy that could not be beaten. At least, that was what I thought they were. That all changed when it came down to the last of them."

"How long ago did this happen?" Mr. Crusader asked the beast knowing that no part of written history spoke of such events as far as he was aware.

"It ended around one and a half thousand of your years ago but it began almost one thousand before that. Mages had lifespans that at times could rival our own. The handful of generations that those slayers went through were almost a dozen decades apart from one another at a guess." The beast said. "At least that is what I assume. Time does not exactly pass normally within this place."

"You have been imprisoned here for all of that time then? Alone?" Mr. Crusader asked.

"Yes. Ever since that final battle." The beast told him. "I was weak, tired and yet the last of the slayers refused to die until I had been defeated. So with the last of his breath and power, he used his ring, the ring that you now wear, to seal me away in this place. I do not know how he did it or how to undo it but that is what happened."

"I'm guessing that I have some connection to the slayers if I am capable of using this ring then? This is obviously something fairly unique if only a handful of mages were able to use them?" Mr. Crusader asked as he looked down to the rock on his finger.

"I do not know. That ring has been absorbing my powers from this place for centuries, it is unlikely that it still works as it used to. You might even say that it has built up an affinity for my kind." The beast said.

"So what do I do with this? What powers does it hold?" Mr. Crusader asked him.

"That is for you to discover slayer. I have already said too much, the ring in unlikely to allow me to go any further. It would be best if you would leave now. I myself need time to collect my thoughts." The beast told him.

"And how would I do that?" Mr. Crusader asked.

"Take off the ring." The beast said and as Mr. Crusader reached for his finger and gave it a tug, the room around him did more than simply go dark as he returned.

In fact.

As the mana that it had absorbed from the dragons breath was towed back to the physical world along with it, the resulting reaction created an unstable pool of energy within the gem.

Which meant that as Mr. Crusader returned. The room around him was vaporised in the explosion that he caused.

4
CONTAINMENT

Whilst Mr. Crusader spoke with the ancient dragon within its void cage, the rest of the world was seeing something far removed from the simplicity of the situation on his end.

Or at least the rest of the world would have seen it, had anyone actually been allowed to look. The SCD and then the ring itself took care of any witnesses. There was nothing left to see.

Instead the masses that had once occupied the bar had been forced to leave. Once by the gunshot that got them out of the door and then again by the two dozen armed soldiers bearing down on them from all sides once they were outside.

A team of SCD operatives. A small team it might have been thanks in part to the limited resources available at the time but one more than large enough to deal with what they had believed to be up against.

Expecting to be bringing in a lone operative. A man with expert hand to hand and marksmen skills but limited magical ones. That was the only perceived threat at the time. Which should have been easy for the men sent to deal with him. Because that team specifically specialized in one key area of SCD operations.

Mage containment.

They never had expected Mr. Crusader to come willingly. He was akin to magic after all. Even if he couldn't truly be called a mage, he was still close enough to have warranted such precautions. That plus his behaviour over his short time away from the SCD had made them more than cautious when approaching him.

He had already slipped through the fingers of multiple team's twice before that point. They weren't taking any chances that time. Not when they had already placed the ring in his finger on site.

Knowing how likely it was for him to run made them speed up the schedule when it came to their plan for him and the ring. If there was a chance that they couldn't hold him long enough to introduce the two of them, then bringing the artefact into the field to force into his hand upon capture seemed like their only choice.

It certainly wasn't their first choice but after an extensive risk assessment and assurances made as to how securely the threat posed by the ring would be contained, it was released into the custody of Agent Mathias. Under the orders of the field commander waiting outside.

But even without the ring they had to take steps to ensure that the plan went as intended. He was after all capable of using basic magic on his own. As long as it wasn't his body actually casting the spell anyway. But still at great cost. The jewels or gems that he used as both a mana source and a method of spell activation were not without their flaws.

Most notably, being that if a human had tried to use one, the harm to them would have been severe if not immediately fatal.

Only a mage was supposed to be able to do anything with them in the first place but it was a well-known fact that on occasion even those who merely carry the mage gene could also make use of them for a limited time.

But these people would have often found only death down such a road had they followed it for long enough. The pain and mental load that a spell would have placed on their bodies would normally have been too much to bear for more than a handful of seconds but Mr. Crusader was different.

He was not a full mage, a generation or two away from it from what the SCD had been able to figure out but he was close enough. Close enough to be able to use the stones, to channel and control the mana within as well as to cast a variety of spells with them but also close enough to remain mostly intact after the fact.

Usually sustaining nothing more severe than a burn mark from the mana reacting with his body after the use of each jewel. More than minor enough to be overcome by the endless benefits that even basic magical abilities could give him. Especially since he had mainly used that power, to kill others with magic light-years beyond his own.

Mr. Crusader was in part human but in others was ultimately a mage. A half step on the evolutionary scale required for him to become a being of magic.

His parents were most likely carriers of the mage gene. Actually they would have both had to have been.

The mage gene is a recessive one. Taking two carriers to allow it to flourish and even then only having a fifty-fifty chance of succeeding in producing a mage.

Most times it takes two if not three generational tried to make a mage. The first allowing the child to carry a stronger variant of the gene and then the next generation, as long as both parents were still carriers, having an increased chance of succeeding from there.

This would continue on and on until the mage gene takes hold in one of the children and from then on, that child would be a mage and all those proceeding him also.

The process could not be reversed or at least not easily.

If a child that was born a mage were to have a impregnation

with a non-mage gene carrying human, the chances of survival were slim but the evolutionary process could be turned around.

That child being born as a carrier only and having to start the evolution to mage hood all over again.

This was what had happened to Mr. Crusader's blood line already.

His ancestor, the knight that gave his life to kill the dragon, had been a full mage. Capable of using magic, generating mana and using the sight. However his son, born to an ordinary human mother, was only a carrier.

Mr. Crusader was lucky that his parents and those before him had been gene carriers. Had they not the ring on his finger would have killed him instantly for not being capable of using it.

But even though he had a stronger variant of the gene, enough to use the most basic forms of magic that there were, he was not a perfect match. For that to have happened, he would have needed mana of his own.

Mr. Crusader had nothing but the innate ability to process spell casting. A hereditary trick of the brain allowing it to take in the required parameters and spit out the sigil sequence for a spell.

He could not actually cast the spell however, for that he would need a catalyst. Such as his jewels. They would take the strain of casting the spell from him and even supply it with their own mana to allow him to survive the process.

But they did not allow him to exist on the same level as other mages. For that he would have needed the sight.

Whilst it was uncommon for a child born in a mage family to be born without the sight it did happen. But for those with only one parent as a mage and the other as a carrier, the sight was an unpredictable inheritance.

However for Mr. Crusader, he had been born from two carriers. The chances of him having gained the sight from this were next to nothing. In fact there have only ever been three humans to gain the sight. And none of them lasted long.

Being able to see something that no one else can perceive or feel marks you with insanity soon enough. And try as they might, humanity has never treated its psychiatric patients well enough o allow them to be reformed back into society. Instead they lock them up and experiment with different sequences of pills until they find something that seems to fit.

So even though he was not a mage in the strictest sense. Having no sense of mana or magic surrounding him and a very limited ability to even feel the stuff, he was still close enough to exist amongst their ranks if not their society as well. Which also made him close enough to have been deemed as much of a threat as the rest of them.

That was why the containment team was there. Because he was a threat not only to them but to the rest of the world as well. Whish explained their orders.

To eliminate if not restrain him upon resistance and to bring him in forcefully if possible. There never was a chance for him to escape them. Not that time.

The SCD had permitted him to have his fun once, ignored the conflict that dawned from their previous capture attempts and even prolonged his unauthorised holiday in an attempt of encouraging him to return. But they were not going to do that again.

Now that they had managed to track his family tree back to that of the knight that had once worn the ring in their possession; he was too vital an asset to them. Someone that they could study and use for a variety of applications and reasons. He was not someone that they would simply allow to slip through their fingers anymore.

However on paper, he was still what he had always been.

A knowledgeable soldier with expert training and years of experience. Basic magical abilities and an understanding of SCD protocol. No more of a combat threat than that of a highly trained killer.

Which meant that in the end he was seen as what he had always been, an eventual but not present threat to their security, not that their personnel. He could not be allowed to continue on in the public world without constant SCD supervision. The level of risk taken by already allowing him to be outside of their influence for such a prolonged period of time had been too high to take again.

That was why the containment team had been sent. Because if they hadn't been there and the soft approach had been taken instead, the odds of him remaining free would have been too likely. And the SCD was anything except foolish. If he had escaped again then he would have never eluded them forever. Because the next time it would be an assassination order with his name on it. Not a retrieval.

But as it happened, as the true outcome of that encounter between Mr. Crusader and the ring placed in his hand was played out; all of them, all of that effort and all of their equipment, training and preparation; was useless.

For as those men entered the bar, watching as agent Mathias and Mr. Crusader discussed his ordered return to employment, as they observed Mr. Crusader placing the ring on his finger, nothing that they could have done would have changed a thing.

Because in the five minuets that he spent communicating with the dragon contained within the void, only a mere three seconds passed for the rest of the world.

Just long enough to witness Mr. Crusader vanish as he was transported to this dimension, seeing the ring that he was supposedly wearing float in the air and glow radiantly as he was gone and just quick enough so that no one had been even the slightest bit prepared for what came next. The fire, the heat, the light and the sound.

The explosion that preceded his return.

An unfortunate result of the excessive energy that the ring had absorbed from the dragon in the void. Normally such an attack would have been converted back into pure mana for the ring to have used to booster its own supply but nothing like that happened.

The ring that existed in the bar and the one in the void were the same. Two objects that were identical and linked to one another existing at the same time in differing points of space. So when the ring in the void absorbed the power of the dragon's breath in the three seconds that it took, the ring in the real world was forced to attempt absorbing the same amount of power; in less than a dozen milliseconds.

That level of power forced into the mana pool of the ring at such a ludicrous rate overloaded its capacity instantly. Forcing the energy to overflow and expand outside of the ring where in reaction to the atmospheric composition of that bar, caused all of it to combust. Brilliantly.

So as Mr. Crusader began to pull of his ring to return to the bar that he had left, the explosion that came before him expanded ever more as the mana of the ring itself was added into the mix. Creating a forceful build-up of flames on par with that of a well-made tactical explosive.

The bar was vaporised in its entirety from this. Not even the foundations almost four feet below remained.

The men both inside of the door and standing just beyond it; the twenty five total that have been in rage of the blast, died almost instantly.

And then as the ball of fire continued to burn for over three more minutes as the ring attempted to contain and control it – expanding slowly the entire time as the ring lost grip on its power – a sizeable response was sent to put a stop to it.

And in the meanwhile, whilst this ball of flames continued, Mr. Crusader found himself stuck. Suspended between the void and the real world by the ring. Kept in a state of condensed time slowing him down enough that in the three minutes that it took, not even a half of a second passed for him.

In a way he had been lucky. Had the ring not accepted him as its new master, no steps to protect him would have been taken. Instead he would have been thrown back into the world with no regard for whether or not he would survive the process.

For the time being he would alive. Kept that way by the ring alone. But as time went on, his chances of staying that way continued to decline.

The mana that the ring was constantly outputting to protect him would not last forever. And even if it did, the fire was not his only threat.

Because down the road from the site of this explosion, came both the men whom would have taken Mr. Crusader into their custody and the man commanding them.

All of them rushing form their position in a well-guarded building down the road to deal with the perceived threat. Instead of him being brought to them for the debrief and reassignment that had been planned, they would instead have to go to him. After they dealt with the ball of fire slowly eating its way through the dirt obviously.

But as the ball of fire began approaching the array of black Sudan's lined up on the path leading to it, it suddenly just stopped. Both in movement and in combustion. Proceeding to begin collapsing within the first few seconds of its halted movement and then breaking down altogether after that.

Dimming and then disappearing entirely as the mana fuelling it finally ran out. The ring holding the fire in place as well as Mr. Crusader in stasis fell to the floor within a moment of it doing so.

Leaving a fully conscious and untouched man standing above it in confusion as he stared at the destruction that battling with the dragon from within the void had caused. Completely unaware that such an event had in fact been entirely avoidable had known how to control the powers of the ring to defend himself rather than leaving it up to the ring itself.

"What the hell happened?" Mr. Crusader muttered to what he

had assumed to be himself.

"My question exactly agent!" A man in a thick black suit said from above the small crater in which Mr. Crusader was stood.

This man then surrounded by even more soldiers from the team that had accompanied him from a local sector to assist with his recovery of Mr. Crusader.

All of them wearing standard issue magic resistant armour and carrying the latest in anti-mage technology. Generation two prototype rail guns. The first working model safe enough for field testing. The fifteen that they carried, being the only working units in existence at the time.

By their weaponry alone, those men were in essence a significantly dangerous and extremely deadly hit squad. Their training qualifying them to take on the most challenging of foes and their guns surely allowing them to claim the victory..

They were most certainly not the simple containment team that they were meant to be. Their commanding officer had lied about that part.

He didn't want a captive, he wanted a specimen. And Mr. Crusader did not need to be alive to fit that criteria.

So as Mr. Crusader looked at the men, realising their confident stances and movements as well as the unfamiliar weaponry that they carried were not that of the lower tier operatives that he would have expected; he quickly came to the conclusion that his chances of making it out of that situation were slim at best.

He would have to be greatly careful going forwards.

His life depended on it.

"SCD identification and rank?" Mr. Crusader asked the man that had spoken in a strong and authoritarian manner. Quickly turning his eyes towards each of the soldiers surrounding the crater that he found himself stuck in as they fanned out to cover all the angles.

"Classified." The man said, grinning slightly as he spoke the word. Feeling glad that for once he had been able to say that aloud. His position in command was still a new concept to him after all.

"Mission directives?" Mr. Crusader asked him.

"Also classified." The man said.

"Authorisation Crusader, Timothy N. Military clearance level seven. In accordance with SCD jurisdiction protocol nine, nine, four dash one section B. I formally request an explanation of your purpose here as well as your rank and name!" Mr. Crusader stated strongly, trying to force the man into introducing himself at the very least.

"Actually your clearance level was eight as of a few minutes ago. But not anymore. And as I said... it's classified." The man told him.

The man raised his right hand slowly after those few short words, waving it towards Mr. Crusader to signal the men stood next to him to act and within a moment of seeing it, they moved.

Three of them. Carrying restraints as the rest of the men repositioned their guns as to not harm them and approaching Mr. Crusader quickly with every passing second.

"What is the meaning of this? I am a Major dam it!. An agent same as you. I have rights! Authority!" Mr. Crusader pleaded as the large metal cuffs were wrapped around his wrists. The men standing around him holding him tight as they forced him to step forwards.

"Under mage containment protocol zero dash fifteen, all those found responsible for the destruction of property or personnel be them civilian or SCD affiliated are to be restrained and brought in for questioning regardless of circumstance. Remember?" The man asked Mr. Crusader as he approached.

And as Mr. Crusader dropped his head in response, knowing that he had no way of arguing with that statement, something else decided to get involved. And whilst it did it with the purest of intentions, they did not come across as such.

The ring couldn't exactly communicate through words in an

effort to explain itself obviously. Not from that distance.

But as Mr. Crusader took his fifth step away from the ring on the floor of the crater, its connection to him, took a firm hold. The sixth step coming next and the pain setting in instantly.

A drilling sensation throughout his body, as though every bone in it were being bored into from all angles. Excruciating and unending pain, forcing him to his knees as he screamed. The sight and sound of a man that none would have ever wished to see.

For in that moment, he was a man, displaying and experiencing pure and unadulterated agony.

Enough to shale any man watching it down to the core.

The men escorting him tried to pick him up but the more they moved him the worse the pain became. The agent arresting him realising that he was in no way faking it by the expression displayed on his face alone and being forced to intervene took a few steps forwards to control the situation.

But as he approached, carrying the mana supressing drug designed to incapacitate and nullify a mage in every way with the intention of using it to knock Mr. Crusader out for the foreseeable future, the ring sensed the threat that he posed.

Realising that if he had gone through with it that its new master would have been taken an even further distance from it, the ring broke its own rules and took it upon itself to help Mr. Crusader more directly.

Summoning him to its side and forcing him out of the hands of the men desperately trying to restrain the screaming man in-between them.

And as he was pulled, forced to fly back down the slope of the crater, the pain went away. Almost instantly. As did the shackles.

They fell from his hands as he moved back, dropping to the floor and staying there as though they had never been locked around him in the first place.

But with it now seeming as though it were Mr. Crusader's

doing, the men surrounding him followed their standing orders to deal with him if they perceived an imminent threat.

So they opened fire.

The ring it seemed, had not seen that one coming.

5
NEW TRICKS

Fifteen men surrounded him. Fifteen expertly trained and trigger happy soldiers surrounded and trapped him. And the fifteen weapons that they carried effectively caged him.

Sixteen men total, only one in command and the others to follow him. Fifteen grunts and an officer. An agent. A man whose name was no longer entitled information for Mr. Crusader to know and a man who was carrying out mission directives that were clear enough to see.

The rank of major and the security clearance that came with it meant little to this man. He was only following his own agenda and using the already existing SCD protocol to his advantage to pursue his goals.

Which in that moment meant only one thing. That if his option to take Mr. Crusader in peacefully had disappeared then his standing orders would have to be carried out. Which in accordance with the SCD protocol, named Mr. Crusader as an enemy combatant. Marking him for execution or confinement. Whichever one was deemed the simplest to achieve.

Mr. Crusader had been seen as nothing more than a threat thanks to this protocol. Not as an officer or employee, nor a mage hunter or expert on anti-mage combat tactics. No. To them, he was no better than everything else that they had killed in the past.

They didn't care.

To them, he was guilty of crimes affiliated to magic. Crimes that to the SCD especially, stripped him of his rights. Both as a human and as an officer under their command. To them, he didn't even exist anymore.

He was believed to responsible for the destruction of the bar and the subsequent lives within. Which in a way was true and would have led him down the same path as any other in his situation if it were but he disagreed.

He understood the orders, knew full well the protocol that they were following but still believed that they were wrong. He was one of them, a fellow agent. Working with and alongside them for almost an entire year by then and still they would treat him as just another mage.

It wasn't right.

He was their superior. His clearance level and rank well above their own and yet they had the orders that gave them the ability to fight him. To view him as nothing but an outcast. A target.

And for as long as he was perceived as a threat, that was not likely to change.

Mr. Crusader intended to do something about that.

Even if he hadn't originally wanted to work for them, even if he hadn't chosen to join them, the SCD was his home now. Its funding, his lifeblood. Its walls his cage and its weapons his shield. But most importantly; its employees, were the only friends that he had left.

Leaving behind a life of killing people in exchange for significant amounts of currency and changing to one of containment and research. Very rarely ever seeing true combat no matter how dangerous the targets might have been.

That was all he knew now.

He had been forced to abandon his previous life. To leave his home, his untrustworthy friends and even his country. But even so, after a year amongst them, he had accepted his new life gladly.

A day to day existence of following orders that he knew never to question and doing only what was expected of him giving him a sense of purpose. Knowing that no matter what the order or why he had been given it that they outcome would be the same. The protection and salvation of his species.

That was his goal. To help out the SCD in any way that they required and to do this knowing that once his tasks had been completed, lives would have been saved.

Eliminating the threat that mages posed and sleeping easy knowing that yet one more enemy of his people lied died beneath the dirt. That was what he thought he was doing. And for him, he would have had in no other way.

But to have gone through all that he had to get there, to do what he was doing and to have been rewarded by having his men stand against him, pointing guns at him and carrying orders that allowed them to open fire on him. Was unacceptable.

Because if he died there, by the hands of the same organisation that he had served, it would have all been for nothing.

Allowing his life of killing anyone who needed killing to become one with purpose had allowed him to feel good about himself. But to have been seen as no better than the people that he had been killing, made all of that worthless.

Spending so much time killing those who would do mankind harm to then only be seen as the same thing made his life meaningless.

To be treated as one of them, to be seen as nothing but another rogue mage responsible for the destruction of property and the loss of lives, angered him so deeply that even the ring sat below him in the dirt was able to pick up on it.

He had worked hard to get to where he was. To reach his rank and to secure his clearance level. Pushed back down and stripped of that over and over again but always coming back up.

He had strived to learn what he had done and to obtain what he now owned. He was not about to let that go. The SCD would never stop hunting him if he had chosen to.

He knew that there was no escaping their reach. Not alone.

There was no way that he would have survived on the run even if he had wanted to. He had to stay, he wanted to stay. But they had opened fire on him already, seeing his actions as that of aggression and not ones that he had been forced into as they were and leaving him to his fate.

He was stood there, wrongly accused and hunched over directly above the ring in the centre of the crater, watching them pull on their triggers.

The prototype weaponry slower and far less accurate than its future iterations but still just as deadly. And with Mr. Crusader without conventional magic and possessing no further gems to be used to aid him, he had no way out.

No way of defending and no way of running.

He was stuck, doomed and marked for death but still, even though he knew his fate and how unchangeable it was, he refused to accept it.

He was adamant that he could still find a way out of that situation, fight up until the end.

Then the guns fired, surrounding him in a ring of blue energy as the weapons discharged their stored up power and altering him within an instant to what they meant, his belief that he could make it out of there vanished entirely.

There were fifteen projectiles in all. Each of which almost impossible to see, hurtling towards him at speeds double that of a conventional bullet and none of them even the slightest inch off course.

He had less than a split second to live after that.

So as Mr. Crusader realised this, curling up in a ball as he fell to the floor, that second passed. The shards of metal approaching him finally arrived and impacted. Every single one of them.

Making contact and tearing through.

But as Mr. Crusader opened his eyes once more to look, confused as to why he was not yet dead, he saw something far different than what had been expected on his end.

A dome. A half cylindrical ball of pure energy surrounding him, protecting him.

A fluid like structure as reflective as though it were made from glass over three metres wide and half as many tall covering him like a shield. Saving him from each and every bullet and it drew near.

And with its walls almost a full foot thick, the projectiles that had been fired slowed and finally stopped once inside of them. Not a single one ever reaching his person. Never even getting close to hurting him.

By some miracle, he was still alive.

"What?" Mr. Crusader said quickly in disbelief. Amazed not only by his apparent survival of his execution but also the large and seemingly self-casting barrier surrounding him.

"Crusader!" The agent in command of the men meant to kill him shouted. "You have not been permitted to live. Drop that barrier. Die with some dignity dam it!"

"What do you expect me to do? I didn't do this." Mr. Crusader told him, opening his arms out wide to signal that he was as surprised as everyone else was as the men surrounding him questioned what they were to do in light of his seemingly impenetrable defence.

The surrounding men didn't buy it through. Firing another volley to test his shield and then another. Forty five projectiles implanted in the barrier and none of them making it through.

The men gave up on shooting after that.

"So you claim to not be the one who cast this spell?" The agent asked him, not believing his words for a second. Knowing that no other mages should have been anywhere near that position to have been able to save him but having to question him regardless in light of his apparent invulnerability.

"How could I? I can only use basic magic and I mean basic. This is light-years beyond me." Mr. Crusader pleaded.

His words oddly reaching the ears of the agent questioning him and sparking some form of realisation within his mind. And whatever it had been, this realisation had allowed him to believe Mr. Crusader's words. At least partially.

"And the explosion that destroyed the building that used to reside here?" Asked the agent.

"How should I know? I put that ring on and for a few minutes I wasn't there anymore. I was in a dark expanse of nothingness, talking with a dragon if you can believe that. I took the ring off again and when I returned this was what I found." Mr. Crusader explained.

"Did you say dragon?" The agent asked him, tensing up greatly in response to his words.

"Yeah?" Mr. Crusader asked in confusion.

"Men! Stand down." The agent said, the men standing around him lowering their weapons almost immediately in response. "Looks like I won't be arresting you after all."

"Sorry?" Mr. Crusader asked him.

"I work as a part of the research team responsible for studying that ring. If you say that you actually survived wearing it then it would look like you belong to me now. Naturally your rank will be lowered accordingly whilst you are under my care." The agent told him as he slowly approached, walking down the slope of the crater and inspecting the thick barrier in front of him.

Pressing his palm against it and running his hands across its silky smooth surface little by little to ascertain its strength and density.

For an apparent soldier, he seemed to know a lot about magic barriers to have been able to do that. From Mr. Crusader's perspective, he certainly looked like he knew what he was doing.

"So what does that mean exactly?" Mr. Crusader asked.

"Figure out how to lower this barrier first. We have things to discuss in private." The agent told him.

"I don't know how to do that." Mr. Crusader moaned.

"I believe that the brightly glowing piece of jewellery at your feet might have something to do with this field. Pick it up." The agent said.

"Glowing?" Mr. Crusader asked as he looked down, finally spotting the deep red light emanating from the ring on the ground and looking stunned as he realised that he had been yet to notice it.

He bent down and picked it up, watching as the barrier surrounding him moved along with it, startling the men surrounding his position greatly as they saw it.

"Now what?" Mr. Crusader asked.

"Put it on obviously." The agent said.

"The last time I did that I disappeared." Mr. Crusader stated.

"Just put it on." The agent repeated.

So Mr. Crusader placed it back on his index finger, only to find that it no longer fit correctly, as though it had grown. Confused, he moved it down to another finger and then another, soon realising that it now could only fit a single digit in his hand. His ring finger.

There was something odd about that.

And upon placing it on his hand, to his absolute surprise; nothing happened.

"Now what?" Mr. Crusader asked.

"So it wasn't automatic... then it must have been activated in response to your fear of death. Perhaps subconsciously or..." The agent muttered as he raised his right hand to his chin. "Try thinking."

"Thinking what?" Mr. Crusader asked, trying to figure out what the agent was getting at.

But as Mr. Crusader stood there waiting for an answer, the

ring released a quick flash of purple light. The next thing that he knew, the ring wasn't there anymore.

In fact, neither was his hand.

His lower arm in its entirety was gone, as was his now torn up sleeve; replaced by a blade no thicker than his hand had used to be but far longer. A sword. One that was physically attached to the rest of his arm. As though it had always been there.

"Uh..." Mr. Crusader muttered slowly as he looked down at his arm.

"What the hell did you just think about?" The agent asked him as he stood there completely weirded out by what he had just seen.

It's not every day that a man's limbs start turning into metal after all. Nor is it common for that metal to be in the shape of a very long and very sharp double edged blade.

"That if the ring sent me back to that place again then I would need some way of defending myself." Mr. Crusader told him as he waved his arm around.

"Does it hurt?" The agent asked.

"No. It didn't feel a thing. Actually I still don't." Mr. Crusader said, running his left hand along the sharp blade in place of right. "I can't feel any part of this."

"Okay, so try getting rid of it. Picture it turning back into your hand." The agent instructed.

"Alright but I don't think that..."

His hand returned to normal then. The blade collapsing and his hand emerging from it, complete with the ring still upon his finger.

"Huh." Mr. Crusader said.

"Now the barrier." The agent told him.

"Right so I just think... collapse the barrier?" Mr. Crusader said with uncertainty, waiting many moments before seeing it happen. The barrier surrounding him, collapsing in, breaking apart violently. Disappearing within moments with a bright flash of light across its surface as the metal shards implanted within it fell to the floor upon doing do.

"Alright. Progress." The agent grinned. "Now if you would hand over the ring..."

The agent held out his hand, waiting for Mr. Crusader to take it off but as he went to remove it from his finger, something interrupted him.

A sharp pain in his head, accompanied by an odd sound, almost like screeching. And when it ended, when he was able to return to thinking normally without the pain in his temples, he found that he had understood what had been said to him.

"I will stay with the master?" Mr. Crusader muttered in confusion.

"What?" The agent asked him, pulling back his hand.

"When I went to the take off the ring, I felt something in my head. When it stopped, I could tell what it had said. Like my brain had translated the noise." Mr. Crusader said as he looked down to the ring in shock.

"Someone told you that they will stay with their master?" The agent questioned.

"Not someone, something. I think that... it was the ring." Mr. Crusader explained.

"It can communicate with you?" The agent asked.

"That's not really it. It's more that I can understand it. I don't think that I can actually talk to it." Mr. Crusader said.

"Ah..." The agent sighed. "I'll let the experts figure that out when we get back to the lab."

The agent turned and walked away from Mr. Crusader quickly as he signalled to the men that they would be leaving at that point, heading back to the cars and driving back the relative safety of the nearest SCD facility to their position.

The rest of the troops and units that would have most likely been readying themselves to leave by then would be needing instructions before long.

It was best to report in before someone starting missing them.

"Wait is that it?" Mr. Crusader asked as he followed.

"The Cornwall Research Division will want to do all the explaining in person. I think it best if we get there as soon as possible, don't you agree?" The agent asked as they both reached and entered one of the ten black vehicles lining the road.

"Cornwall? As in England?" Mr. Crusader asked, one of the other men turning the key and staring the engine as they spoke.

"Sector Fifteen, basement level four." The agent told the driver as he looked back to the passenger seats for conformation. "Yes, England. You know another Cornwall?"

"No it's just... why England?" Mr. Crusader asked.

"What do you have some history there or something?" The agent inquired.

"Operational history, nothing personal." Mr. Crusader explained.

"Oh, I see. Well it's because that's where the ring was found. About two months ago now. Dug up in a sealed room below what we now believe to be the ruins of Camelot." The agent said.

"I thought Camelot was a myth?" Mr. Crusader asked quickly.

"Not anymore." The agent told him.

"So we're in for a long flight then?"

"Not exactly, I'll explain it as we go." The agent said.

"And we are?" Mr. Crusader asked.

"Second Lieutenant Gabriel Dunning. Clearance level five, head of the Cornwall Research Division." The agent said as he held out his hand to shake with Mr. Crusader.

"*Second* Lieutenant? In charge of a research team?" MR. Crusader asked.

"Something wrong about that?" Lieutenant Dunning asked.

"Not at all." Mr. Crusader said as he grabbed the hand of the Lieutenant to shake it. "You must be something special to have your own team."

"Not really, my father is, I have him to thank for my position.

Now I've introduced myself, what about you?" Lieutenant Dunning asked.

"Apparently I'm now Major Timothy Crusader, Clarence level seven, no, eight. Former Tactical Recon and Mage Elimination Division. American Branch based out of Sector Nineteen." Mr. Crusader introduced himself as the car finally made its way back onto the main road and drove along it.

"Ah, the recon unit eh? And Sector Nineteen would make you a mage hunter. So a sniper I assume?" Lieutenant Dunning asked.

"Correct." Mr. Crusader told him.

"Yes well you didn't strike me as a close combat type. Too well centred, quite focused as well." Lieutenant Dunning stated as the car continued rolling in unison with the others following it.

"So I am to report to you now, *Lieutenant*?" Mr. Crusader asked.

"I am head of the department from a military standpoint. It is for my superiors to decide but my guess is that they will want to keep me in charge. You may end up getting a demotion when we arrive. It will most likely be on paper only though, taking your rank away so quickly after giving you it might not be possible." Agent Dunning said.

"Well it wouldn't be the first time." Mr. Crusader shrugged.

"Really? Forgive me but I am only slightly familiar with your record. I still had much more to go over by the time that we arrived. That and a large portion was classified above my clearance level." Agent dunning said.

"Yeah there were a few incidents that worried the higher ups. I should have been a Colonel by now. But you know, bad behaviour, heroism and unauthorised elimination methods and all." Mr. Crusader explained.

"Well you can rest easy when we arrive, my department has a lot of freedom in many areas. You can thank my father for that as well. So I doubt that anyone will have reason to discipline you. It's not like I have a direct superior to answer to or anything." Agent dunning told him.

"Wait, so you work independently of the military? How did you manage that one?" Mr. Crusader asked.

"We're a research team, the military doesn't have jurisdiction over us unless they need it. And... well my father did that as well." Lieutenant Dunning explained.

"Dunning right?" Mr. Crusader muttered. "So then your father would be... Vice Chairmen Dunning?"

"How the hell do you know that?" Lieutenant dunning asked furiously, knowing that Mr. Crusader should have had no knowledge of the identity of council members.

"We've met." Mr. Crusader explained.

"Oh... is that so?"

"Unfortunately. He didn't seem too happy to have a lower level operative in his company at the time." Mr. Crusader told him.

"That's every council member I'm afraid. No matter who you are, if you don't have rank, it's almost like they shun you just for being near them." The Lieutenant recounted.

"Personal experience I assume?" Mr. Crusader asked him.

"Every time I visit my father it's the same thing but anyway, let's move on. I assume that you have other questions than ones about my personal life?" The Lieutenant asked to try and change the topic.

"Yeah. What exactly is it that your department does?" Mr. Crusader asked.

"Other than uncover ancient magical artefacts of British origin and study them, we have recently discovered that this ring of yours holds a lot of secrets and seemingly a lot of power also. For now, our focus has been on one thing. Dragons." Lieutenant Dunning explained.

"Why dragons?" Mr. Crusader asked.

"Well they were believed to be myth or legend but when we found that ring, the texts that it was locked away with superficially, all pointed to the same thing. That it was used for if not built for killing them. Which I suppose would make you something of a Dragon Slayer now." Lieutenant Dunning said.

"Funny, that was what the dragon called me." Mr. Crusader muttered.

"So you spoke to it and it spoke back?" The Lieutenant asked him with excitement and intrigue.

"More the other way around but yes, that was what happened." Mr. Crusader told him.

"Interesting, so you..."

A large explosion emanating from one of the cars following theirs interrupted Lieutenant Dunning as he spoke. The light of the fires and the shockwave from the blast altering the driver and the man sat next to him almost instantly.

"Car three is down!" The soldier said, turning the vehicle violently and pulling the hand break to be able to see what was happening but that idea whilst good on paper, was almost suicidal in practice.

It was already too close by then.

"What the fuck is that?" The man in the passenger seat asked loudly in shock and fear.

"My god, it's huge!" Lieutenant Dunning said.

"And it's the same one that I spoke to before. Soldier! Drive now!" Mr. Crusader ordered, the driver placing the vehicle into gear and stomping down on the peddle violently upon a moment's notice.

The towering creature in front of them with a car beneath its foot and another in its teeth, staring at them sinisterly the entire time.

It would seem that a chase was about to begin.

After all, Mr. Crusader had let the beast out of its cage. It was bound to want to thank him in person for doing that.

THE LAST DRAGON SLAYER

6

THE CHASE

The mouth of the beast opened slowly. The crumpled remains of the black vehicle inside dropped to the ground in a display of raining fluids, blood and wreckage within an instant as it did so. The men inside most likely dead if not beyond saving already and the weapons carried by them almost certainly useless for those who remained.

The remaining vehicles now rushing to slam on the breaks and set up a perimeter behind the creature and the one car in front of it facing the wrong way entirely.

Whatever was to happen next needed to be well planned and precisely executed. The risk of failure was far too high for it not to have been.

For as the beast stood there, one foot out in front of it to secure its balance on the uneven dirt below and head held high in both confusion and suspense, everyone watching was quickly able to ascertain what it meant.

They could see, the men in the cars behind and the two in front, that the beast did not intend to make the first move. In reality, that decision had been left to them purposefully. It was waiting to see how they would react before it responded. And what they chose to do next, would shape the course of those next few minutes entirely.

There was no room for error.

"Crusader..." Lieutenant Dunning said quietly, turning to him for answers.

"Yeah?" Mr. Crusader asked, not taking his eyes off of the thing for even a second. Staring directly at it with both fear and intrigue as he questioned what it would do next. Expecting that his death would be both swift and painful were it to gain the upper hand.

"Any ideas?" The Lieutenant whispered as the men sat in the front two seats awaited the reply as well. All four of them frozen in shock and unable to do anything out of terror.

"You expect me to know something that you don't?" Mr. Crusader asked rhetorically.

"As it stands you have the most contact with this thing. You might." Lieutenant Dunning said.

"Are you asking me as the more experienced agent or as your superior?" Mr. Crusader asked him in confusion.

"Seriously? You're pulling rank now?" The Lieutenant snapped, turning his head quickly towards Mr. Crusader who in turn looked at him and the both of them making a grave mistake by doing that indeed.

For as their heads were turned, the men behind the beast still climbing out of their vehicles and grabbing their weapons from the trunks, the dragon saw the opportunity to strike in their distraction.

Pouncing forwards with force, approaching the idle vehicle quickly and with almost deadly precision. They had only moments to react.

"Drive. Now!" Mr. Crusader shouted as his eyes finally noticed the movement. His head snapping back to the dragon and entire body jerking forward as he gripped the seat in front of him to pull himself closer to the front of the vehicle.

The agent in the driver's seat listening and reacting to him quickly, placing the car into gear and slamming down on the peddle. The car jolting forwards within an instant as its acceleration began.

The car and all four of the men within it heading directly towards the beast within moments, terrifying them greatly as they approached it. That was not the direction that either of the passengers had intended to move in.

"I meant away!" Mr. Crusader stated as they grew nearer.

The right leg of the beast slamming down onto the ground, narrowly missing the car as the driver steered to the right of it, weaving in between all four of its legs as they continued. Barely grazing past its teeth as the head came flying towards them upon reaching its feet.

"This was a terrible idea." Lieutenant Dunning remarked as they continued driving, passing the hind legs of the beast and now driving beneath its swinging tail.

A tail, that was soon to be coming their way.

With both speed and force it moved. Like a whip it waved and within an instant it had gone from several dozen meters in the air to less than a single one off of the ground. But it did not go further.

Upon nearing the top of the car, something had thankfully managed to prevent its approach. Something that had been taking its sweat time to happen.

The men from the vehicles that the driver was hurrying towards, finally opened fire on the creature.

Their prototype rail guns still no match for the thick hide of the beast but more than enough to have harmed it. At least slightly. Grazing it just barely enough that the beast could be distracted by their impacts. And as they gradually chipped away at the scales on its back, the anger of the dragon grew greatly.

Turning its head towards them in hate as it watched them fire over and over again until their magazines were depleted. And with the car that it had meant to destroy now nearing their position as well, it would seem that there was only one thing left for it to do.

Attack.

Raising its entire body into the air as it turned, supporting its weight on its hide legs whilst moving, pointing its head directly at its targets and opening its mouth as wide as it would go. The vibrant colour of the energy beam exiting it lit up the night sky as it drew closer.

Then within a moment, everything was over.

The head of the dragon went from right to left as its body hit the floor, the beam racing out of it and impacting the ground beneath the men attacking it, vaporising them and the vehicles that they had cowered behind. Leaving nothing but smouldering rock in their place.

But as it approached Mr. Crusader, as the final few nanoseconds passed before it would have hit his car that had diverted to the left and driven along the line of cars now non-existent behind them, it was gone.

No beam, no fire and no dragon. It just disappeared as though it hadn't been there to begin with. But the destruction that it caused; that remained.

Something didn't quite seem right about that.

"Stop the car!" The soldier in the front passenger seat shouted as he looked out of the window in shock.

And as instructed, the car stopped quickly.

The driver pulling the break and halting all movement within a second.

"What the fuck are you doing?" Lieutenant Dunning asked.

"It's gone sir. I can't explain it but it's gone." The driver said in disbelief.

"Impossible. It was just there a moment ago." Mr. Crusader stated, a sharp pain hitting his temples a second after saying that before he had gotten the chance to look.

"Major?" Lieutenant Dunning questioned.

"It's returned to the void. It must have ran out of mana to

sustain itself here." Mr. Crusader said, relaying what the ring on his finger had just told him, gripping his head in pain as it continued to speak. "It will return eventually though."

"The ring tell you that?" Lieutenant Dunning asked.

"Yeah." Mr. Crusader said, shaking his head as the pain subsided. "It could try speaking a little quieter though."

"Then we got lucky. Now, soldier." Lieutenant Dunning said, directing his words at the driver.

"Sir!" He responded.

"Contact command. Request a tier four containment team as well as search and rescue. After that get the closest General on a secure line to me as soon as possible, I'm going to need to report this personally." Lieutenant Dunning ordered.

"Understood sir." The soldier said, grabbing the radio on his shoulder and beginning to search for an open channel.

"Crusader, with me. You. Grab your weapon and follow behind us." The Lieutenant said to the other soldier in the front of the car.

The three of them excited the vehicle quickly, the soldier grabbing his rail gun from the trunk as instructed and Mr. Crusader following the agent closely as he had been told to. Approaching the wreckage that lied before them as each second passed.

Flames and shrapnel were everywhere. Littering the road and the dirt either side of it without end. Then every few feet, an arm or leg would appear as well. Too many of them to count.

"So that was a dragon?" Mr. Crusader said ominously.

"Far more powerful than I had imagined." The Lieutenant said as he turned to look over everything that there was to inspect. The researcher in him taking over in light of the threat dispersing.

"It didn't look like your guns did much good. But I doubt that anything more conventional will have an effect because of that though. You have anything more powerful?" Mr. Crusader asked the agent.

"No. Those guns were prototypes, first working model off the assembly line actually. I'm not even supposed to know about them. I doubt we have anything else that would compare." Lieutenant Dunning told him.

"So the next time that the dragon appears..." The soldier following the two asked.

The pain in Mr. Crusader's head quickly returned.

"You want me to fight it?" Mr. Crusader said loudly as he looked to the ring on his finger. Another wave of pain coming only moments after the fact. "What do you mean grow a pair?"

Obviously the ring didn't approve of his reluctance to fight. It was both the purpose of its existence and Mr. Crusader's allowed use of it for combat with a dragon to occur. For him to have been unwilling to do so, was not acceptable.

"Major." Lieutenant Dunning said impatiently.

"Yes?" Mr. Crusader asked quickly.

"If the two of you are just about done, you should remember that you will be answering to me soon enough. If you are to fight it, you will not be given the choice." He told him.

"Yes I know that." Mr. Crusader said in disappointment as the fires continued to burn around them.

Then the footsteps came. Quick and heavy. The soldier that had been left in the car approaching with excessive speed.

"Containment and salvage teams are on the way. And Brigadier General Mordoa is on his way via..." But the solder did not manage to finish his sentence in time however. The General appeared right at that moment behind him.

By means of a teleport.

"Lieutenant. Major." He said, greeting them through smile.

All four men stood to attention quickly in salute. They had most certainly not been expecting him to appear as suddenly as he had.

"General, sir. I was not expecting you to be sent in person

upon my request, nor did I expect to be seeing you here so quickly but arriving by teleport is a bit..."

"Not to worry Lieutenant, the mage that was used is trustworthy enough for such a basic task. I've known him for years in fact. By this point it would be insulting not to trust him." The general said.

"Understood sir." Lieutenant Dunning said in acceptance.

"Crusader, good to see you. Been a while since you escaped my facility has it not?" The general asked, keeping both arms behind his back as he stood there in the mud waiting for a reply.

"Almost four months sir. Yes. You will have to forgive the circumstances, I had wished to explain my actions more formally at a later date." Mr. Crusader told him.

"I already understand why you did it and quite frankly I agree with your choice. Now would someone like to explain this mess? I heard something about a dragon and stopped listening after that. So I am expecting quite the story." The General told them.

"Well sir I doubt that you will believe me but here I go anyway." Lieutenant Dunning said, beginning his explanation of the events moments later.

And whilst the General might not have understood or believed all of it, he at least had a much clearer picture. A clear enough picture in fact, to start making some very major decisions.

Just not the ones that anyone had expected him to make.

THE LAST DRAGON SLAYER

7
CONTROL

Whilst understandable, bringing such a high ranking member of the SCD to the site of such a major defeat was hardly the wisest choice. Especially considering what said individual saw fit to do once on the ground.

Any other solder would have made the same decision though. With his low rank and suggestively lacking experience it was likely that Lieutenant Dunning simply sought guidance from the General. But that wasn't exactly what he received.

"Lieutenant." The General said with force and authority, alerting Lieutenant Dunning to attention within an instant.

"Sir." He responded.

"Effective immediately Major Crusader here will be replacing you as head of the Cornwall research team currently focusing on this disaster." The General ordered.

"But sir..." Lieutenant Dunning went to say.

"No buts. I gave you ample men and weaponry to carry out your mission here and look where that got you. In light of your limited success in finding a man who can actually use the ring I will refrain from placing you before a disciplinary committee. That is final." The General told him, the rescue crews and more of the SCD's forces finally beginning to arrive as the conversation went on.

"Sir I appreciate that I may have the higher rank here but I am by no means qualified to run a research department. I have never worked in that field. I strongly suggest that Second Lieutenant Dunning remain in his position or at least beneath me in an advisory one." Mr. Crusader pleaded, fearful of how much his career would be effected once placed in a position of not only power but significant responsibility also.

"Major you are in no position to be making suggestions." The General said sternly, putting Mr. Crusader off the idea of attempting to persuade him any further almost instantly.

"Ye... Yes sir. I understand." Mr. Crusader said quietly.

"And I sincerely doubt that it will be anything that you cannot handle. Considering that the top research subject will be yourself for some time going forwards this should be no more challenging than a walk in the park." The General stated.

"Wait does that mean....." Mr. Crusader hurried to ask before his words were taken out of his mouth and answered before he had even gotten half way.

"That you will have limited authority despite your position, limited access to facilities and no means of contacting anyone that is not directly connected to your department as all other personnel subject to testing are? Yes it does." The General told him.

"Understood. Sir." Mr. Crusader told him.

"Sir with all due respect are you out of your freaking mind?" Lieutenant Dunning asked in a tone of jest despite his sincerity.

"Second Lieutenant Dunning!" The General said with force. "It is because of you that thirty three men lie dead. Because of you that we have lost almost all of our prototype weaponry meant to deal with events like this and because of you that we now have another class one threat to deal with at this time. I would watch how you speak around me going forwards."

Lieutenant Dunning stopped talking after that. The threat that the General had given him but not said in as many words was not one that he wanted to challenge.

For both as a general but an SCD employee as well, that man had access and control over some very dark methods of punishment. Methods that the Lieutenant would not be exempt from had the General wished to put him through them.

"Sorry sir, did you say two class one threats?" Mr. Crusader asked.

"Yes son. As of the past few months we have been unable to communicate with the magic world. To the best of our knowledge, no one has been seen to exit its boards in some time and all whom have entered, have not been seen again." The General explained to him. "Whist this development is not an immediate threat, not having any sign of what is going on in there has led our superiors to view the silence as a preparation of war. They were at one point debating the idea of attacking first."

"Off course. All this time of hunting mages, I always suspected that the information gathered on them had come from somewhere. We had people on the inside. Didn't we?" Mr. Crusader asked him.

"Members of the Magic Council that thought it best to have us deal with their assassination targets for them. Yes. Either way, we still got what we wanted. Less mages to have to eliminate later." The General explained.

"I see." Mr. Crusader muttered.

"Lieutenant, I trust that you will do best to forget ever hearing that." The General told him quickly.

Lieutenant Dunning nodded but said nothing.

Then as the silence began to dawn, a car approached them. Large and robust like those previously lost during the short battle and painted black almost identically to the others as well. And as it stopped, a man immediately stepped out.

Wearing the same plain military uniform that the privates standing guard over the men were and steadily walking towards the general as the seconds passed.

"General Mordoa. Sir!" The soldier said, standing to attention with his right hand in salute as his left kept firm hold of the rifle dangling from his shoulder.

"Captain Leema, your timing is impeccable as always." The General said as he turned towards the man. "At ease."

"As ordered this car is here to take you and the prisoner wherever you wish to go. No questions, no paperwork." The Captain said, turning to the right and pointing his arm out towards the vehicle.

"Wait. Prisoner sir?" Lieutenant Dunning questioned.

"A bit of a strong word but close enough is many ways. Captain, detain the Major here will you." The General ordered as he stood in place smiling ever so slightly.

"Yes sir." The Captain gladly responded, lowering his arm and walking over to Mr. Crusader with force as he stood there in shock of the words that he was hearing. Not for a moment understanding why it was that after all that had happened he would still be under arrest by the organisation that he worked for no less.

But as the Captain reached his rear Mr. Crusader had no choice but to comply. Placing his hands together out in front of him as large zip ties were fixed around his wrist and walking forwards upon the commands of the Captain pushing him with the rifle he carried from behind.

And as they reached the car, the general seated next to him in the rear of it with the captain in the driver's seat, Mr. Crusader had only one thing left to do.

Ask questions.

"Respectfully sir and quite understandably, I have to ask. What the fuck are you doing?" Mr. Crusader asked loudly.

"Headquarters Captain." The General said as he closed the door and relaxed into his seat.

"That's a three hour drive sir." The Captain stated.

"So get going." The General said.

"Yes sir." The Captain confirmed, reaching for the hand break and stepping on the peddles accordingly to begin moving the vehicle for which he was to control for the next one hundred and ninety four minutes.

"Now, what exactly were you saying Major?" The General asked Mr. Crusader.

"Sir, I am failing to see a point in my current position. To the best of my knowledge I have done nothing that would require restraints." Mr. Crusader said.

"True. But in order to get unauthorised personnel into headquarters I would either have to wait a weak to get you temporary security clearance or take you in as a captive for interrogation or trial. I am merely keeping up appearances." The General said.

"General... Steven. Come on. The last time that I went anywhere near headquarters I was being shot at. I doubt that I'm going to be able to just walk in." Mr. Crusader said.

"Unfortunately we do not have a choice. Something that you and the Lieutenant mentioned before has created a great sense of concern for me. The council members as well once they hear about it." The General said cryptically.

"What sir?" Mr. Crusader asked.

"The void." The General told him.

"Sir?" Mr. Crusader asked.

"It is not for me to say and not for our present company to know about." The General explained.

"Apologies General." The Captain said.

"No need son, just keep driving." The General said.

"So you are taking me there to what? Talk to the council? No agent that I know of have the authority to even request and audience, let alone get one." Mr. Crusader asked.

"No, none of them do. Because no field agent has ever had clearance. In order to get in, I will have to convince my superiors first. Coincidentally and quite fortunately, almost all of my higher ups are currently in headquarters dealing with the ongoing situation in the magic world. We won't have to go far." The General explained.

"What exactly do we know about the condition inside the boarder's sir?" Mr. Crusader asked him.

"Not much. Ten months ago we attempted to contact one of our inside men after noticing a complete lack of communication in the few weeks prior to that. We managed to reach him for a few moments but what he told us did not make much sense." The General explained.

"What did he say sir?" Mr. Crusader asked out of curiosity.

"That the darkness was coming. The transmission cut out after that and we have been unable to contact him or anyone else inside since. The council and most others agree that this is most likely a prelude to war and as such most of our forces have been positioned in the surrounded countries since this message was received." The General said.

"If I may sir, my money is on that angel guy. From the stories, he would be the most likely man to start a fight with us." The Captain said.

"Appreciated Captain but that is above your clearance level and from our intelligence he is not strictly speaking an enemy of mankind. At least not yet." The General told him.

"Understood sir." The Captain said.

"So we have no idea what's going on in there and you can't tell me why I'm being arrested until we reach headquarters then?" Mr. Crusader asked.

"That's about right." The General told him.

"Then I have one more question to ask. How did you know why I had left? I can understand the man sent to apprehend me figuring it out but for that information to have made it up the chain…"

"I already knew." General Mordoa said.

"Sorry sir?"

"When you were positioned under my command with a very limited and obviously falsified history in your file, I did a lot of digging to figure out who you were. So when you left, I did some more digging and came across the name of the man who killed your family in the obituaries of the local paper. You knew that someone had covered up your disappearance right?" General Mordoa asked him.

"Sir, I never thought that it had been yourself." Mr. Crusader told him.

"I thought it best to give you some time. So I made you invisible for a while. But then you never came back. Everything that happened after that was your own fault." The General explained.

"Thank you sir. And just to be clear, what else do you know about me?" Mr. Crusader asked in intrigue.

"A lot more than you would want me to disclose. There are some gaps but I know everything up until you turned ten, a few pieces of information before you turned eighteen and then most of what came after that. Including your little incident at headquarters." General Mordoa explained.

"And this information is..."

"Secure and physical. No copies and no digital record. Don't worry about it." The General told him.

"Alright then. If that is all we have to talk about I will rest for what little time I can." Mr. Crusader said as he too gave in and relaxed into the relative comfort of his seat in preparation of the long drive ahead.

Then as the twenty fifth minute passed, Mr. Crusader almost managing to drift off to sleep in an attempt to sober up once awake again, the sound of ringing hit his ears. The in car communication system, the cell phone to be specific, receiving a call.

"Sir, I have Lieutenant Dunning on site of event zero one."

The Captain said as he inspected the display in front of him to authenticate and recognise the caller.

"Patch him through." The General said.

The call clicked on almost instantly.

"Lieutenant?" The General asked.

"Sir, we're making good progress here. A perimeter has been set up and media blackouts have been enforced. Containment teams are collecting the wreckage and masking the mana traces but regretfully, there were no survivors. I take full responsibility for that." Lieutenant Dunning reported.

"As you should. Now what aren't you telling me? I can hear the fear in your voice." The General asked him.

"Well one of our science teams sent to investigate the magical component of the threat arrived five or maybe six minutes ago and they almost instantly found something quite disturbing sir." Lieutenant Dunning explained.

"What?" The General asked him.

"In their words. A problem." Lieutenant Dunning said.

"Explain more Lieutenant." The General said.

"Well the mana signature of the attacks as well as that of the atmosphere are identical. There's no doubt about it, they come from the same place." Lieutenant Dunning told him.

"The dragon and the ring share the same mana signature?" The General asked him.

"Not just that, the same exact frequency. Sir, if I had to guess, I would say that the dragon is what's powering the thing. It's the only conclusion that would make sense." Lieutenant Dunning said.

"Thoughts Major?" The General asked Mr. Crusader.

"Well the ring was able to absorb one of the earlier attacks so that's possible I guess. Like fighting fire with fir sir, you cannot protect against yourself." Mr. Crusader told him.

"That's not all sir." Lieutenant Dunning said.

"Go on." The General told him.

"Well the dragon, it didn't just appear out of nowhere." He said.

"No I doubt that." The General said.

"We've found something worrying about how it did appear sir. A mana type that we have never seen before, seeping into everything that it touches but not reacting to any of it and according to these readings, it's more potent than all other sources. And I mean all." Lieutenant Dunning reported.

"What's so worrying about that?" The General asked.

"The only locations that we have detected it are directly beneath where the dragon was stood and sir..."

"Yes?" The General asked in anticipation.

"In the direction that you are now headed. Whatever this stuff is, it's following you. Perhaps even latched on." Lieutenant Dunning surmised.

"So are you saying that it's tracking us?" Mr. Crusader asked.

"No, more likely it is coming from you in some way. Whatever form of connection your ring shares with the space that the dragon is being held in perhaps? We don't have the data to be sure." Lieutenant Dunning theorised.

"What are you saying exactly? Is this mana type dangerous?" The General asked.

"The mana itself no. What it is most likely to be used for, yes." The Lieutenant said.

"Lieutenant?" The General asked.

"I think that this mana, is a residual effect from the ring venturing back and forth from the void. It is possible that it is even an after effect from the doors being left open. Like a key." Lieutenant Dunning said. "My theory which is so far shared with two of the members of the science team standing here with me is that when the dragon broke back into our world, it used this mana source as a means of aiming where it landed. It is highly probably that when it shows up again it will do so as it did before. Right on top of you."

"Ah... Shit." The General sighed. "Good work Lieutenant, report to me again when you know more."

"Will do sir." Lieutenant Dunning said as he disconnected the call.

"Captain." The General said.

"Sir?" He asked.

"Change of plans. Take us to Sector Fifteen. Containment entrance. Inform the research chiefs that we're going to need them to put their new toys into action. Looks like we'll be needing a sealed room." The General ordered.

"Understood sir. Estimated time to arrival is fifteen to twenty minutes." The Captain said as he suddenly turned off of the road that they were on to go down a dirt path leading back towards that which they desired.

"General?" Mr. Crusader asked.

"Looks like the council will have to wait. We need to get you on ice. Almost literally." The General explained.

So the three of them continued on their journey for the next nineteen minutes as expected and upon arrival made their way inside of the facility almost instantly.

What came after this however, was most interesting indeed.

8
WHITE ROOM

The distinguished General – a forty nine year old Mr. Steven Mordoa – had been working with the SCD for most of his long militant life. Being nothing more than a determined yet underachieving sailor's son before that.

He had given them a grand total of thirty one years of his adult life by then. And other three of his adolescent one.

Thirty five years as a soldier and all but one of them had been in their service. Anyone who knew this would have suspected him of being completely complicit in their actions by then. But he was anything but.

Submitting to their will and reason for more than three quarters of his entire existence without any sense of when it would end had taught him what he had needed to know to survive under them. To keep his head down and nose out of it. That was how he had kept his freedom in check.

He might not have agreed with everything that his superiors and employers were up to but he didn't exactly want to face the consequences of going against them. Instead he did as he was told and kept up appearances wherever he could at appearing to be the loyal solder that he had always been.

He certainly understood how to survive.

Having gone from nothing more than a simple front line grunt to a respected and revered desk General had allowed him to see and experience many things over the years.

Many tragedies and secrets that those under his command were not permitted to know about and even some that his superiors had forgotten about. Allowing him to gain many answers to questions that he should not have known how to word as well.

An understanding of both science and magic beyond any SCD soldier and entirely unreachable by anyone else. Knowledge of world politics and how easily it could be influenced. And knowledge of just how willing the SCD were to work with the very mages that they were supposedly at odds with as long as it served a purpose.

Had he the choice, he would have forgotten most of this information. It would have made his life a little easier to bare. But one thing remained throughout his life. One piece of information, one wisdom that could not be ignored. That all magic, no matter the source, is undeniably deadly. Even that which he was meant to trust.

And whilst most men in service to the SCD mainly dealt with mage related threats and mysteries, there were those like him, whom had seen so much more than that. The truth behind what many of the subdivisions of the SCD were really up to and how devastating this truth would have been had the rest of the world known of it.

In reality he knew enough to have made him one of the most cautious Generals still in action. The others were already deceased. Because they, like him, had known too much for the SCD to allow them to continue in their service. However unlike them, he had kept his mouth shut so far.

As long as he did that, the threat that he posed would be seen as contained. But as soon as he stepped out of line, and like so many others before him it was inevitable that he would, there would be no record of him ever existing.

No obituaries, no coroner's report and no burial.

It would be a swift and off the books execution leading to incineration. The orders for this action coming direct from the top of the chain and through word of mouth only. There would have been no way to prove it.

It would be made so that no one, no journalist and no citizen, would ever be capable of finding him or the information that he had once known. He would just be gone.

So he kept his head down and ensured that his actions were as in line as they could be. Lest risking his own life in the process. So when it was discovered that the man in his custody could in some way pose a threat to others as well as himself – despite how much he had not wanted to – the General decided that taking him to address the council was no longer an option.

Knowing now that the mana signature either coming from Mr. Crusader's ring or following it was in reality a sort of anchor if not just a means of tracking him, made him more than merely concerned about spending any more time than was necessary around him as well.

That was why he did it. Out of fear.

Where Mr. Crusader had once been a trusted subordinate of the General, he was now seen as no more than a threat. Exactly as everyone else believed him to be.

The ring on his finger refusing to leave his side without risking his health and its potential for destruction without measure. There was no way to remove it without losing use of it and there was no way to trust it without a severe amount of risk being placed on those in the vicinity of it.

So if the scientists working in the Cornwall Research Division truly believed that destroying it was both impossible and ill-advised as they had reported in the early days of its testing, then the General was left with only one other choice.

To contain it.

But a magic that strong, with a man latched onto it as well, made that a tricky task indeed. Needing enough room to safely house a person but a secure enough one to protect against its mana would have been impossible several months before this but at the time, a new invention that was perfect for this situation had just entered the testing stage.

Mage containment cells. Three feet of steel surrounding it on all sides with isolated life support and water systems. And of course, prototype Anti-Magic Field Generators bearing down on all inside of the room from above.

It was theoretically impossible for anything, any mana or spell in existence, to survive in there. And in theory, the ring would be included in this as well.

So when the car finally arrived at the facility that it had been instructed to reach, using the back entrance and venturing underground within moments of entering it, Mr. Crusader soon discovered exactly how people like him were treated by the SCD. Not only was he a now a true prisoner in more than just a sense but a class five threat just by wearing the ring as well.

Had he been a mage instead of a human, that might well have made him a class four. Only one point off from the Athereon himself.

No one person was deemed as dangerous as he was at that time. It was unheard of for any human or mage to have ever been more than a class three and he was getting close to that already. But after all, that ring was an unknown magical artefact with undefined abilities. And he did have a dragon on his tail as well.

"This was please." A Sargent Collings told Mr. Crusader as they continued though more and more securely locked doors on the way to the testing facilities.

General Mordoa had disappeared off within seconds of their arrival, Mr. Crusader had been following the Sargent ever since. Anxious of what awaited him the entire time he was almost shaking by the time that they reached the room. But never did he expect what he found. Nor could he have.

"Sargent. Sir." A man in a plain black shirt and neatly ironed trousers not fitting any recognisable uniform that Mr. Crusader was aware of said as he saluted the Sargent upon his approach.

It wasn't a military uniform, there would have been insignia's or flags at least but it didn't seem to be civilian clothing either. Somewhere between perhaps but unrecognisable nevertheless. It did however, have something somewhat worrying on the side of it.

Not a name or set of stripes but a number. Complete with a hashtag as well. From this alone Mr. Crusader had been able to deduce that this man was no mere soldier, he was attest subject.

As for what test he was a part of, was anyone's guess at the time.

"Corporal. At ease." Sargent Collings told him as he saluted back, watching as the man returned to his somewhat stiff stance even though it was supposedly a more relaxed one. "Open it."

"Sir." The Corporal said, turning to the massive eight by four foot steel door behind him and entering a code on the keypad sticking out of it before also providing both fingerprint and retinal scans as well.

It was anything if not secure.

And as the light on the screen went green upon authentication of his access codes and I.D. he pulled down on the handle, the bolts within the frame unlocking in an instant before finally allowing the door with slowly swing open on its hopefully robust hinges.

The door did weigh several tonnes after all.

The light bouncing off of the walls from the other side of it hit Mr. Crusader quickly as it creaked towards him. A blindingly bright and almost natural one at that. Added in with the perfectly white padding on all walls and the lack of windows made it clear that this room was dual purposed.

Fit to secure any prisoner sure but also to disorient and

confuse them. Perhaps even gradually torture them as their minds slowly went insane once the natural sleep cycle was broken under the constant light.

But as Mr. Crusader realised this he also knew that he had no choice but to enter. Whatever the ring was doing, be it intentionally or not, that room was supposedly designed to negate it. In theory, making it almost entirely inert. Safe.

Just one problem though.

The ring could tell.

A sharp throbbing pain hit the legs of Mr. Crusader within a second of him approaching the room, forcing him to fall to the floor and express his pain.

The Sargent had been warned that something like that could happen based on what the ring had done to him back at the bar and went to pick him up as a result. An attempt; that led to nothing but failure.

The ring sensed his approach as well, forcing Mr. Crusader back with speed and impacting the concrete wall as he landed on the other end. It had no intention of entering that room willingly.

Mr. Crusader however, knew the risks of not going through with his orders. The lives that would be in danger if steps were not taken to stave off the dragon's next strike.

He wasn't about to give in so easily.

So he picked himself up, forcing his legs to move through the constant pain, through the sensation of a thousand knives slicing at them whilst a fire roasted them and he kept moving.

One thought constant in his mind the whole time.

That his situation in that moment was no different than the last time. When he was just a child.

At the age of twelve he broke both of his legs rock climbing, under the supervision of his newly adopted mother that is – as unofficial as that title might have been – but on her way down to help him, climbing down the cliff as fast as she could rather than go on the three mile walk down it; she too fell from its face

She wasn't as badly hurt as he had been but that did not mean that she had gotten off freely. Instead of a broken bone she received a serious knock to the head that led to her becoming unconscious within moments.

With no one around and the both of them being three miles from the closest point of the reserve with phone service, Mr. Crusader had to make the choice. To bare his pain and then some in order to walk in a straight line for the next two hours and dragging his mother behind him as well.

He thought about this as he made4 his way towards the white room awaiting him. Realising that if could do that back then, then what he was up against now was nothing in comparison.

Pain was an optional experience. He just had to ignore it. So he took another step.

Then as the pain worsened, as it grew to his core, winding him as though he had been hit by a hammer in both lungs, Mr. Crusader hunched over and took yet another step forwards despite the feeling of this sensation. Keeping the image of him walking through the uneven terrain for those two hours with his bones cracking apart more and more after every step in his mind to motivate him to continue.

And it most certainly worked.

The men surrounding him, the Sargent, Corporal and random scientists, technicians and cleaning staff just going about their business, observed the ordeal from a distance. Frozen in the shock of what exactly it was that they were seeing.

But Mr. Crusader kept going. Reaching the door once more and knowing that only three more steps awaited. The ring attempting to throw him back from it again but to no avail as he gripped onto the handle of the door and kept holding on as his legs and lower body flew out behind it as though he were flying through the air.

But even so, even under so much force and no matter how much the ring tried to stop him, he pulled himself forwards along the door, inching his way into the room little by little as the excruciating seconds went on.

But even with all of his effort, he could not go on. His energy depleting quickly and the force pulling him overwhelming every muscle that he had to use.

But he was close enough. Close enough to be given a push. And push they did. The Sargent and the Corporal, forcing the door closed with all the energy that they had to spare and little by little getting Mr. Crusader ever closer to the nullifying effects of the field within.

All he had to do was get his finger over the threshold; that would be enough to make it stop. And as the door closed, Mr. Crusader still clinging onto it for dear life as the ring continued to try and force him back, it finally happened.

His hand entered the field coming from that room and that was it. The force being applied to him disappeared and his body fell to the floor. The pain vanished and for the smallest of moments, everything seemed fine.

The door closed behind him as he scurried into the room and locked almost instantly once it did. Then for only five seconds, everything seemed normal. But as the sixth arrived, everything was anything but normal.

But he had been ordered to stay in that room. That was exactly what he was going to do. He was anything but disobedient. So no matter what he had to endure whilst in there, that was where he was going to stay. Nothing could have broken a man with his kind of will power.

"LET ME OUT!" A screeching voice said to Mr. Crusader.

Not coming from his mind but from the air surrounding him. Almost as though another person was there with him but that was impossible. He was quite obviously alone.

Then he looked down to the ring and saw it. A glow unlike the others. A green energy slowly draining out of it and seemingly being absorbed into his hand. Colouring in his veins and racing up his arm like a sickness.

"Who said that?" Mr. Crusader asked as he stared down at his hand in fear of what such discolouration would mean. Unaware that any form of magic could even do such a thing to the body.

"SILENCE. Let me out of this cage!" The voice said again. Like a hundred screaming children in unison. All of which identifiably female in gender. It was a strange presence indeed.

Strange not only because the voice existed, most likely the ring that it was truly coming from, but that its tone would infer a sense of gender to the supposedly inanimate object on his finger.

"I can't. I'm in here for the safety of myself and everyone else." Mr. Crusader told the voice.

"Major who exactly are you talking to in there?" General Mordoa asked through the speakers in the ceiling. Microphones and several cameras were up there too.

Nine feet up and no way of reaching any of them.

"If I'm right and not entirely insane, drunk or being pranked; the ring sir." He replied.

"I thought it caused you great pain when it spoke. Why do you seem so calm?" The General asked.

"Look to my arm sir, I assure you that I am anything but calm. I would guess that the adrenaline in my system from the effort it took to get in here is masking my emotions somewhat." Mr. Crusader said as he raised his right hand and pointed to it with his left.

"Yes I saw that, good work son. I looked like you had done that before." The General told him.

"I went through something similar, yes." Mr. Crusader replied.

"The marks on your hand and arm, do they hurt Major? Do they feel hot or sting at all?" A new voice suddenly asked.

"Not currently. If anything, they feel numb" He explained.

"How far has it spread?" The voice asked again.

"AS FAR AS I SAY IT WILL unless you let me out!" The voices screamed at him, inaudible to those in the observation room and proving without a doubt that this was still going on in his mind like before.

However with the absence of any pain when it spoke, the ring had either been severely weakened by the field or it was interacting with his mind in an entirely different way.

But Mr. Crusader ignored it and took off both his jacket and his shirt to see how far the green veins had reached by then.

Luckily only his upper arm and shoulder at the time, no further as far as he could tell.

"Just my shoulder." Mr. Crusader said.

The silence that followed took several seconds to end.

"We would like you to take off your belt and use it as a tourniquet. As far up the arm as you can get. At the very least it will slow down the spread." The voice said, seemingly a scientist or doctor of some kind.

So Mr. Crusader did as he was told to and applied the basic tourniquet using his brown leather belt. Once there, it did seem to slow the spread but even so, it was still worrying that it existed in the first place.

"So any idea what this is?" Mr. Crusader asked.

"YOUR DEATH!" The voices laughed.

"We have seen something similar before. It's a corruption of mana, similar to a plague actually, normally spread from person to person but it can pop up on its own. It only happens in there when the field is set too high. Give us time to adjust it for you." The voice said.

"So this field. Prototype anti-magic tech right? I've read a few reports but that was months ago. Mind telling me how it works while I'm here?" Mr. Crusader asked.

"A network of delta wave emitters and mana crystals that in tandem with each other create a field of high density mana, kind of like a form of static, which when configured correctly prevents the casting of spells and can even drain most other mana types from the bodies of those effected." The voice told him.

"Is that safe?" Mr. Crusader asked.

"As long as the subject is only exposed to it for less than an hour a day or so. We are still working on a more practical and permanent application." The voice said.

"Alright." Mr. Crusader said, looking to his watch to figure out when he would be due to exit.

"Okay, that should be better. How does it look?" The voice asked.

So Mr. Crusader looked down to his shoulder once again and whilst the substance was no longer moving, perhaps even turning a slightly darker colour, it was not going away.

"It's stopped spreading but it's still there." Mr. Crusader told him as he gently poked it to see if he had regained full sensation yet.

"That will have to do. Any more and lower level mana might start flickering in and out of existence. That would be painful if not completely devastating." The voice said. "I'm Davis by the way. Chief science advisor to most SCD facilities."

"Good to meet you, oh ominous voice of the sky." Mr. Crusader said with a chuckle. The alcohol obviously having at least a small effect with his sense of humour.

"Enough with the flattery, please." Davis replied in laughter.

"Gentlemen if we could get back to the matter at hand." General Mordoa said. "Now Major, is the voice still there?"

"More like voices, a hundred or so speaking in unison. But not for a few seconds now no. Almost like it shut up. Which is greatly appreciated." Mr. Crusader told him.

"Well it is possible that with these new settings whatever mana source the voice was coming from has been better nullified now" Davis suggested.

"A shame, I would have liked to question it." General Mordoa said.

"Respectfully sir, it is a ring. What knowledge could it possibly have?" Mr. Crusader asked in confusion.

"No matter what form it might take, give an item enough mana of sufficient potency for long enough and it has a tendency to develop a consciousness. Depending on how old it is, that ring could know a lot of things." Davis said as he caught onto what the General was getting at.

"Well if you want to know more you should probably connect the Cornwall team in on this call. They were researching it after all." Mr. Crusader suggested.

"Good idea Major, we'll have them patched in within the next few minutes." General Mordoa said.

"So what now then?" Mr. Crusader asked.

"No idea. This was as far as my plan went." He said.

"Not much of a long term solution sir." Mr. Crusader said.

"Well we didn't have an awful lot of choice in the matter. If that dragon had come back through over our heads on a highway or god forbid whilst in headquarters it would have been a very tragic and very public event." General Mordoa said.

"Yes, I see your reasoning. Regarding that, are we still detecting the same mana signature?" Mr. Crusader asked.

"According to my instalments, which are not perfect mind you, no mana source of any kind is entering, exiting or inhabiting that room. You're cleaner that most humans right now." Davis told him.

"Well, I'll be here until you need me then. Just dim the lights a little, I'm going to make use of this bed while I can." Mr. Crusader said as he laid down on top of the plain and surprisingly comfortable sheets.

"You want us to just watch you sleep?" General Mordoa asked as the lights dimmed upon request.

"If you want sir. You could always look away or turn off the monitor. I'm not going anywhere for at least an hour am I?" Mr. Crusader told him.

"Yes well..."

"And unless you specifically need me, I suggest just leaving the scientists to themselves. I don't know them and have never read any of their research. I would only slow them down if I got involved now. Just fill me in when you figure something out." Mr. Crusader said.

"Forgetting the tone... that sounds good Major. I'll check back in thirty. Do not fall asleep!" The General told him.

"Yes sir." Mr. Crusader said with sass as the General walked away from the console in front of him, venturing off towards the conference rooms on the floors above in anticipation for the call from the Cornwall team.

A call, that was most enlightening indeed.

For some anyway.

THE LAST DRAGON SLAYER

9
CONFERENCE CALL

On the short ride up the elevator to the conference rooms three floors above the testing chambers where Mr. Crusader was to reside, General Mordoa came across quite the interesting fellow in the corridor across from it.

Carrying a pile of paperwork the size and weight of a small child and steadily increasing in pace with every step. Obviously hurrying towards whatever destination awaited him and taking no care to avoid anyone on his way there.

Forcing the others that he encountered during his journey to either quickly step around him or jump out of the way as he bumped into them whilst continuing on. He would have kept doing this too, had he not come across the General during his travels.

"Make a hole!" The hasty man said, failing to avoid the other man stood in his way before hitting him head on and dropping a large amount of his paper on impact. "Oh just great!"

The man leant down to begin picking up the sheets instantly, not looking towards the General for a second other than at his boots and lower trousers as he stared at the floor. Completely failing to notice the uniform that the General wore or the stars upon it as he rushed to grab everything.

"You not going to help?" He asked the General, expecting him to have lent a hand at the very least if not apologise also but he stayed silent. Angering this man greatly as he did so.

But the man picked up the last of his paperwork and stood back up after that, prepared to give whomever it was that he had ran into quite the earful upon doing so. An action that would not have gone down well had he gone through with it.

"Do you have any idea how import this work is? All of you gru... General Mordoa. Sir!" The man said, standing to attention rather than saluting in light of his excessive load.

"And you are?" The General asked impatiently as he placed both his hands together behind his back in an effort to maintain his composure.

"Stevens. First Lieutenant Dale Stevens. Strategizing correspondent of field operations out of Sector Fifteen." He said, relaxing slightly into a state of anxiousness as he calmed his greatly angered nerves.

From busting anger to child-like fear in the face of such a powerful man. Not exactly what he would have considered to be relaxing but close enough under the circumstances. He didn't feel like shouting anymore.

"Lieutenant Stevens... yes, I've read that name before. On several complaint forms. You don't seem to be getting along with everyone here that well. And by that I would have to mean everyone, for me to have read even one of these reports means that you are quite the trouble maker. As it seems, that might be true." The General told him.

"A misunderstanding I assure you. My job is to recommend the best course of action during field missions. My reactions when my recommendations are ignored do not go over well with everyone." He said.

"Yes, one or two of the reports said something about... excessive verbal outbursts. To your direct superiors no less.

Regardless of that, explain yourself soldier." The General ordered.

"Sir forgive my lack of attention to my path, sir. This paperwork has to be filed by hand once a month and I had been pulled away from doing so after that dragon fiasco earlier. My deadline was quickly approaching and one more slip could see me reassigned. I do somewhat enjoy this job sir." The Lieutenant said.

"Clearance level Lieutenant?" The General asked as he realised that information of the exact circumstances regarding the dragon had already been deemed need to know.

"Eight sir." He said.

Eight being a clearance level well above what it would have needed to be to know about the dragon was the correct answer by a wide margin. Strictly speaking, the majority of the details pertaining to the dragon attack earlier were only a level four matter but by General Mordoa's orders, it was not a matter that could be allowed to be spread through word of mouth. So if this lieutenant knew about it, then he was not cleared to do so but required to.

The General no longer had cause to hold him any further. Bumping into a man was hardly an event that was worth any form of punishment. Even a verbal warning would have been pointless.

"Very good soldier. Carry on." The General said, stepping out of his way against the wall behind him as the Lieutenant continued on.

"Thank you sir." He said quickly as he turned the corner that the General had bumped into him from, making his way down to the archive room quickly from the looks of his path.

With him out of the way, the General continued on his march also. Reaching the elevator at the end of the corridor he was in and entering it at the press of a button. A Major Tobias waiting for him patiently inside.

"General Mordoa. Sir!" He said, saluting within moments of

the doors opening.

"Major..." The General paused for a moment as he saluted back and allowed the Major to relax after the fact. "...Tobias, Human Resources. I remember we met at the new mage engagement course last May. Top of the class weren't you?"

The Major grinned as he heard those words and waited for the doors of the elevator to close before speaking any further. The nature of their discussion being above the clearance level of most staff whom might have overheard them as they walked past the elevator gave grounds for some discretion on both their parts.

"Sir. I have been sent on request of Colonel Borret who in turn sends his apologies for not being here in person. I understand that there is to be a conference call held soon, regarding the confidential matter that occurred roughly sixty eight minutes ago. If you will allow, my superiors have asked that I sit in on that conversation." The Major said.

The General thought it odd that Colonel Borret, a rather close friend of his, had been unable to attend since he was not currently on any deployment that he could think of but it wasn't likely to be a problem.

The Colonel was only supposed to be there as a recorder in a sense. Keeping track of what was said during the call and to convey that information to both the scientific and defence boards after the fact so that they might stay on the same page.

A Major taking his place shouldn't have been an issue. He obviously had the required knowledge and clearance level if he had been sent in the first place.

The General had little issue in allowing him to tag along.

"Not at all Major. It will be a good change of pace to have someone different sit in on one of these calls. Don't tell him I said this but Colonel Borret can be a bit of a drag at times. I trust that you will not be following in his footsteps?" The General asked in humour as the elevator ride continued.

"An opinion that many of us share sir. I agree and I will do my best to ensure that I do not." The Major replied.

"Very good son." The General said, waiting for the elevator to finally stop moving and then stepping out of it as the doors opened moments later.

"This way sir." The Major said, taking the lead and walking towards the conference room waiting for them up ahead.

And after three more minutes of walking, they finally arrived. The call already set up and the cameras already on. The men whom had done this, nowhere to be seen.

They obviously hadn't had clearance to remain after the fact.

But in place of these men stood a room set up exactly as it needed to be. A large table fit with no less than twenty chairs and a microphone in the centre precisely as expected. All of which facing the eighty inch screen built into the wall at the other end.

The callers in question, already displayed upon it. All twelve of them.

Eight from the Cornwall branch, two from downstairs in the testing chambers and another two scientists from the site of the first incident.

All of them civilian scientists. None of them military.

An entertaining conversation was bound to follow.

"Gentlemen... ladies." The General said as he took his seat at the top of the table. The Major closing the doors and drawing the blinds upon entry before then taking his seat next to the General as well.

"General." One of the men closer to the screen than the others in the Cornwall branch said.

"This call if being held to discuss how best to proceed with our current situation. That being both the condition and possible threat of Major Timothy Crusader currently in test chamber nineteen and the eventual threat of this dragon. Is that clear?" General Mordoa asked them.

Each man and woman present on the call responded in acknowledgement within the following few seconds. None of them doing or saying anything of note during this time however.

"So who wants to begin?" The General asked.

"I believe that should be me." Davis said quickly. "At current the condition of Major Crusader is stable and contained. No energy signatures other than our own can be detected and the corrupted mana in his system is slowly dissipating."

"And before his entry, what of the mana signatures then?" A small man in a white lab coat from the site of the first event asked.

"Unclear. This mana signature is so foreign that our instruments can barely detect it. It might not even be what we would conventionally call mana. This could be an entirely new source of energy." A co-worker of Davis said as he turned from the console in front of him to look to the camera whilst speaking.

"From our findings I wouldn't say new. It's old. Perhaps we cannot detect it correctly because it predates everything that we can." A scientist from the Cornwall team said.

"Is that possible? For a mana source older than what is already in our database to exist? The oldest source that we know of is one that we have had repeated dealings with before is he not?" The Major asked.

"The... so called Athereon entity? Often referred to as the angel?" Davis asked.

"That is accurate yes but as he and his magical abilities have evolved over his lifetime, so too has his mana. Its pure form might well still be one that we have never seen." Another scientist from the Cornwall team said.

"Or it could simply be that this mana source is older than even he is." A different scientist from the same team said.

"Or that this ring is somehow special. Perhaps with it not being biological, mana sources that would have otherwise been incompatible are capable of existing within it." The small scientist from the first event site said.

"All valid theory's but we have no way of being sure." Davis said.

"Am I the only one here who hasn't heard of this Athereon?" One of the female members of the Cornwall team staying mostly quiet asked quietly, perhaps in embarrassment.

"Ah, I should have asked this first. What exactly are each of your clearance levels?" Major Tobias questioned, realising that he should have done so well before asking his previous question.

"Ten." Davis said.

"Nine!" His co-worker shouted.

"Eight" and "Twelve." The two men on site said.

"Three of us are a six, two are seven and the other three are clearance level nine last I checked." The apparent leader of the Cornwall team said.

"Information on the subject known as the Athereon is strictly a matter for those with a clearance level of nine or above. Anyone below that clearance level would do well to forget everything that they have ever been told about him." General Mordoa said sternly.

"Yes sir." The leader of the Cornwall team said.

"Now, we have established that this ring is either exceptionally old or has a mana source that we have never encountered before. Perhaps an entirely new one. How does this help us exactly?" Major Tobias asked.

"If it is new or one that we have never encountered before then it doesn't. But if it is an old one, one that predates everything else, then that does help us." The leader of the Cornwall team said.

"How so?" General Mordoa asked.

"Well it will tell us where it came from." Davis answered.

"So...?" Major Tobias asked.

"Understand where it came from and we understand more of its past. Perhaps even what it's capable of." Davis said.

"From what we have been able to dig up, it did not originate in Camelot, perhaps not even England. Even though that was where we found it." The leader of the Cornwall team said.

"No it most likely came from a land distant from it. According to the admittedly untrustworthy written reports on the subject, it was a kind of family heirloom before it was locked in the vault of Camelot. Perhaps even going back upwards of ten generations." Another scientist from the Cornwall team said.

"Passed down through the supposed Dragon Slayers you mean? That is what this dragon called Major Crusader is it not? The report wasn't too detailed." The smaller man on the event site asked.

"It is. So what do we know of this subject? Do we have any proof that they existed, or that this dragon actually communicated with Major Crusader?" The General asked.

"Do we need more proof than an actual dragon sir?" The taller of the two men asked.

The General did not answer such a stupid question.

"Well from what we have heard from Major Crusader's reports, they might have done but that is the only source I have at current." Davis said.

"Actually I can offer proof." One of the female scientists at the back of the room in the Cornwall branch said quickly.

"Go on." The General said.

"Forgive the rough translation but I would like to read to you from the diary of a knight who according to this served under both King Arthur and his father Uther as well." The scientist said. "I killed my third today. My third Dragon Lord. The first two were slain during battle at the side of my king and the third, in service to the prince.

I do not know what magic made these men so powerful but they were unlike any sorcerers that I have ever seen. We lost hundreds of men the first two times. The third, he simply gave in.

But I do know this. If they hadn't been as old and weak as they were, I would not be here now."

"Do we know the name of this knight?" Major Tobias asked.

"Not as of yet, no. It isn't like someone to speak of themselves in the third person in their own diary. But he spoke of killing three of them and at great cost. It stands to reason that there might have been more." The same scientist said.

"So if this is the case, if there were upwards of four Dragon Slayers living at a time, what happened to them? The last time I heard of a mage family dying out without our intervention was back during the great plagues." The small man asked.

"Nature." Davis said.

"How do you figure.?" General Mordoa asked.

"Well if the roll of Dragon Slayer is passed from father to son then it makes sense that eventually the responsibility died out, not the family tree itself. Perhaps through war or by accident but if the fathers were unable to pass the knowledge and responsibility on, maybe due to having daughters rather than sons perhaps, then it would explain why they disappeared without dying out. Major Crusader is after all just one of the living descendants of the ancestral Dragon Slayers, there are bound to be more somewhere if we looked." Davis clarified.

"Yes I agree. But without knowing their names or the names of their spouses and children, it will be hard to track any of them down. And even if we do, we only have the one ring. The others have likely already been destroyed or lost by now. Not that I can explain how that happened." The leader of the Cornwall team said.

"What of the dragons themselves then? Major Crusader spoke of thousands existing in the past. Why is this the first we are hearing about them?" General Mordoa asked.

"We aren't." The taller man on the event site said.

"Explain." Major Tobias said.

"Think about it. Throughout history, in fact in almost every civilization and culture, the mythology of winged lizards that could breathe fire is a constant trend. China, Japan, Iceland, Britain, Africa. Everyone has a word for them and everyone seems to have encountered them. The thing that you have to realise, is that most of these countries and civilizations had no contact with each other for thousands of years and yet a lot of these stories appeared at similar points in history. As though they were all seeing the same thing at the same time." The man continued.

"So dragons have been here all along and we have just missed them? Ignored them? Chosen not to believe?" General Mordoa asked.

"Perhaps. It isn't like we have ever found the corpse of one." Davis said.

"There would have to be an explanation for that. A beast as big as a dragon does not disappear easily." The leader of the Cornwall team said.

"Okay. So the ring is old. So old that it emits an entirely new mana signature. There used to be more than one of them, carried down through the ages by the various Dragon Slayers of each generation and there were at one time upwards of one thousand living dragons.

Is there anything else?" General Mordoa asked.

"Nothing entirely helpful sir. We have questions, a lot of them, no real answers though." The leader of the Cornwall team said.

"Well let's move on then. How should we proceed with dealing with this situation then? General Mordoa asked.

"Other than somehow figuring out how to permanently contain the ring or kill a dragon sir? I have no idea." Major Tobias said.

"And without understanding more about what it can do we can hardly use the ring against it can we?" General Mordoa sighed under his breath.

"No sir, I doubt it." Davis said. "Even rail guns couldn't do more than scratch it. We are ill-equipped to fight it."

"And we are ill-equipped to capture it." The leader of the Cornwall team said.

"Honestly without the full and clear picture, we can't make

any real decisions." Major Tobias said. "This is beyond what Sector Fifteen was intended to handle."

"What about Sector Twelve?" The co-worker of Davis asked.

"On deployment." General Mordoa told him. "But how exactly would an army help us here? The idea is to contain this mess not make it public."

"Then we're out of idea's. This might be beyond what we can deal with. What about sending a request to the mages?" The leader of the Cornwall team asked.

"Even if we could get a hold of the Magic Council how likely are they to listen?" Major Tobias asked him.

"They aren't. In all the history of the SCD we have never asked them for anything because we know that they would never say yes. Like it or not we are on our own." General Mordoa explained.

"Then what of the mages we have in custody? Perhaps a magical assault would have better luck." Davis said.

"Then we might as well send Major Crusader. Let's face it, we aren't capable of dealing with this until we understand it. So let's move on.

Tell me everything that we know about the void." The General said, the jaws of everyone connected to the call dropping as their heard the words.

"The void is a subject requiring a level fifteen clearance level. Not even my boss has that." Major Tobias said.

"Temporary clearance can be granted to any agent or SCD employee provided that the requested material is connected to their current assignment." General Mordoa, a man with a level eighteen security clearance, said.

"Yes sir, it can." Major Tobias said, turning back to the screen as he closed his mouth from the shock. "You heard him."

"Right." Davis nodded. "Everyone who isn't Greg needs get out now!"

And whilst it wasn't visible from the camera, the sounds of many racing footsteps could quite clearly be heard after the fact.

He obviously hadn't been as alone as General Mordoa had assumed.

"How many people were in there with you Davis?" General Mordoa asked.

"Ten, maybe fifteen. I don't regularly count my team members, only a few of them are any use to me." He replied in a slight amount of humour.

Meanwhile, everyone in the Cornwall branch were rushing to move things around. Pulling out notepads and entire folders of paper from the cupboards and throwing them on the table as others closed doors and pulled the curtains.

Obviously they knew a lot more than they were supposed to.

"So what do we know?" General Mordoa asked.

"Sir, almost everything that we have uncovered in the Camelot vault has mentioned the void in some way. Most only just in passing but some in detail. Someone alive at the time obviously knew a lot about it." The leader of the Cornwall team said.

"Only what I heard from the report given by Major Crusader and Second Lieutenant Dunning." The short man on the event site said.

"Same here." Greg, the co-worker of Davis said.

"Start talking then." General Mordoa said, not fully realising the full extent of damage that that particular can of worms would unleash.

Or in reality. The truths that it would unleash.

Mr. Crusader was about to be thrown into a world that he was rather ill-equipped to handle. But after his time working for the SCD. That was a common experience.

It was a pity that they had to disturb his sleep to tell him. Another thirty minutes or so, and he would have been well rested enough to fight at his best for hours to come.

As opposed to the state that he was forced to fight in anyway when the time came.

10
THE VOID

For countless years the SCD had sought it. The place that was to be the answer to all of their problems and the door that once open could lead to so much more than that. The chance and the potential, for every ambition that they had ever had to become reality.

They like many before them chose to call it, the void.

A seemingly theoretical space existing parallel to the one that they already inhabited. Often referred to as imaginary space or perhaps even an entirely different world by some. But despite all the beliefs, all the theories, the data and study; none had ever been able to answer the question.

Did the thing really exist?

If true, if a place of infinite bounds existed just beyond the reach of human imagination and grasp, then proving its existence stood to be a trying exercise indeed.

How can you see something that is invisible, touch something that is without form or detect that which is not truly there? How was anyone supposed to reach the conclusion that everyone else desired? How were they supposed to find it?

A space so well removed from reality that it might as well have been a different dimension all together but so well connected to it that it was as much of everything surrounding it as the atoms that formed it.

A place, invisible to the eye, unreachable by car, plane or boat and untouchable by man but one that is ever present and constantly out of reach. Proving that such a thing was actually there should have been impossible.

The technology to get there didn't exist, it couldn't. There was no way to detect it or to control it. And much like air, it was just there. Nothing could be done about that.

The understanding required to even fathom such a place was beyond that of most. Even the most revered and respected scientists of the world would have been stumped to even propose as thesis on how such a place could exist. Let alone one that would suggest that it actually did.

Humans barely understood basic quantum mechanics at the time, getting their heads around such a thing as the void should have been impossible by comparison.

A race of beings still reliant of fossil fuels and electrical power to run their civilization. One constantly at war with one another over land, religion or power. One that had yet to even scratch the surface of the universe of possibilities laid out before them. A race of beings like that would have been the last one expected to understand such a place.

Let alone find it.

But despite how hard the scientists of the world had tried over the decades and despite how astronomically unlikely it was for anyone to succeed; someone had already beaten them too it. Almost two thousand years prior.

For it was not those amongst the modern age that had discovered the void. Not those of science or technology, understanding or knowledge that had proved its existence either.

In the end it was those who had lived through the Dark Age that had seen such a place. That had documented their findings from testing it.

They just didn't know what they were talking about at the time.

"Are you trying to tell me that one of the main goals of the SCD has been achievable all of this time? That it's already been done?" General Mordoa asked in disbelief, trying his best to stay on the same page but finding himself firmly stuck at the idea that several generations worth of work had been finished before it was even begun.

"Yes sir. The void, also known as imaginary space, is something that we at this point can say without a doubt actually exists, but is also somewhere that humans have been before. I'm sorry to say, that we've been beaten to it." The leader of the Cornwall team told him.

"So the thing that almost every physicist, astronomer, mathematician and general scientist working for the SCD has been trying to do, whether they knew about it or not, was already done?" The taller man on the site of the first event asked.

"Eighty years of work, stuck at the beginning when someone else had already found their way to the end?" Davis remarked in more shock than he had harboured in a very long time.

And whilst the other more scientific minds tried to understand at least some of what they had been hearing, General Mordoa was finding his realisation of what this revelation meant far more challenging.

He had spent a large portion of his career with the SCD hearing of the possible uses of the void. As a prison, a source of energy, a dumping ground; the list went on.

The SCD had sought a way of utilising such a potentially world changing space for decades and the General knew first-hand how far they would go for information on it. But now that they had found it, a possible answer so many of their worries, he almost feared to what end this new found space would be used for.

The SCD had the potential to do good, on occasion that actually did but more often than not their actions could be seen as menacing or even evil. And now they had just been given proof that a place existed where they could make anything in the world disappear.

The General had his doubts about that part.

But as it dawned on him that just because they could say that the thing was real did not mean that they could get there he soon relaxed a little. The world wasn't about to fall apart yet at least.

So as he thought more on the subject, he found himself just as equally shocked by how much the others on the call seemed to know of this top secret experiment. None of them had clearance levels required to have had such information. Obviously someone had been talking.

Any other general might well have made it his mission to find out who.

"Can someone just explain what the void is exactly? My understanding of the more exotic scientific marvels is a bit lacking. Actually non-existent." Major Tobias asked.

"Not surprising." Davis remarked under his breath, not realising that he had been heard.

"Sir, the simplest explanation that I can give is that the void is all around us. Like air, we cannot see it or touch it but it is always there. However unlike air, it is limitless. An expanse of nothingness, like an empty universe of sorts, that exists beyond our understanding of physics and time. Truth be told, there isn't a explanation that I can give that would be dumbed down enough for someone without a serious scientific background to understand." One of the younger members of the Cornwall team tried to explain.

"So in essence, similar to how magic can be used to place a larger space inside of a smaller one, when we open the door to this place, there will be no end to it?" The Major asked.

"Not exactly but close enough I guess." The leader of the Cornwall team said.

"So what all of this means, is that the void not only exists but is a place that we can get to. One that we can visit?" General Mordoa asked them to clarify.

"While the place exists I doubt that we can actually visit it. Not with human technology." Davis said.

"Yes, the power requirements to emit a field such as the one that these documents suggest, the fact that it would double every hour that it remained open; no reactor or power plant on the planet could provide that much energy." The leader of the Cornwall team said.

"Then the only way in is through the use of magic?" Major Tobias asked.

"Yes and no." The co-worker of Davis, Greg, said.

"Right, if it took ten mages to open it for just a handful of seconds the first time, the amount of mana required to keep it open for minutes or even hours would be beyond every mage alive." One of the more silent men on the Cornwall team said.

"Then it would be no different than using them like batteries. They would die from the strain within seconds. The loss of life to make this possible goes far beyond acceptable or even reasonable limits." The leader of the Cornwall team continued.

"How much mana are we talking about here?" General Mordoa asked.

"Well according to this and again the translation isn't perfect, ten sorcerers were commanded by the king – presumably Uther judging the date – to open the great gate as to banish the prisoners of the land inside. Once there they will meet there end at the jaws of the last great beasts. The dragon for which we can neither defeat nor calm." The Cornwall team member furthest to the back said as she read from her pile of paperwork. "It goes on to say that a great wall of flames were observed to appear before this gate closed and then that the sorceress holding it open – quote – gripped their skulls in pain as their eyes bulged and ears bled. Falling to the floor and ceasing to breathe once there."

"They were feeding their prisoners to it?" The shorter man on the site of the first event asked.

"In an effort to keep it from attacking them by my guess." The leader of the Cornwall team said.

"Then even back then, the mana signature that anchors the dragon to the ring was still active? It was able to break through even without someone wearing it?" Davis asked.

"What I said earlier about the last of the Dragon Lords being killed referred to an event that happened before this one. I would guess that the ring was already in the vault at the time so that could be true." The woman at the back told him.

"Then how did the dragon find its way into the void in the first place?" Major Tobias asked.

"Through great sacrifice." The quieter and less engaged female member of the Cornwall team said.

"Please explain." General Mordoa said.

"The material that we found with the ring spoke of how it was acquired. That its previous owner, who was most defiantly a Dragon Slayer from the stories, was said to have been in battle with the last of the beasts. One far stronger than the rest. But when the knights of Camelot, along with their king, set out to arrest this man for treason and the use of magic, a great light was seen in the distance. A light that enveloped an entire town and left a large crater in the ground.

I would think that this dragon was fighting the last of the Slayers and through his actions or its own, was thrown into the void when this light appeared.

Needless to say the man that this ring belonged to was never seen again. Nothing that we have found even mentioned his name." She continued.

"Perhaps it was a last resort. A move made in effort to contain the beast when the Slater fighting it realised that he couldn't kill it?" The leader of the team proposed.

"Locking it away in the void would have killed him. Opening it at all would have done the same thing actually." Major Tobias said somewhat hesitantly as he continued struggling to keep up.

"Perhaps it did, he was never seen again after all." General Mordoa said.

"Then even though this place exists and we can get there in theory, it remains impractical to do so then?" Major Tobias asked.

"If it is true that even ten mages could not hold it open for more than a few seconds then no, it is anything but practical. Not if we intend to use it for what the council suggested." General Mordoa said.

"How does any of this help us exactly?" Davis asked. "Don't get me wrong, it's amazing that we can call the void a real place but considering our current dilemma how does this help?"

The General looked down to the table in front of him and sighed. Placed both of his elbows on it and his hands together before resting his chin on top of them. He had spent so much time talking of the void and the possibility of its uses that he had almost forgotten the reason behind why he was even in that room to begin with.

The purpose of that call was to bounce ideas around and get a clearer picture of their situation as to find a way of dealing with it. Something that all of them were yet to do.

"It doesn't." Major Tobias said.

"Does anyone have any ideas?" General Mordoa asked, hopping for at least one suggestion from someone but receiving no response at all.

Everyone had theories, ways that they thought would have been best to deal with the dragon and the ring on Mr. Crusader's finger but they had no proof that they would work to back them up. And as scientists, without proof they were unlikely to even admit that they had an idea to begin with.

The silence that dawned in that moment quickly grew unbearable before long.

"Sir I believe that our situation is beyond what we can handle. Especially without a better understanding of it. We have no idea what it would take to kill a dragon, let alone imprison it. The more that I think about this the more I have to consider recommending that the council be contacted directly. This situation effects the entire organisation, not just our sector." Major Tobias admitted to the General.

"We bring them in on this and we'll lose all control of it." General Mordoa told him.

"Do we even have any control now sir?" The Major asked him honestly.

"Maybe." The General said. "Davis, Connect Major Crusader in on this line, it's been long enough by now. He's had time to think things through."

Davis turned to his keyboard and began typing almost immediately. Then within seconds, Mr. Crusader was back on the line. Unprepared for the heavy conversation perhaps but the only qualified person to answer any of the questions following that moment.

"Major?" General Mordoa asked.

"Still alive sir." He said quickly.

"Good." The General replied. "Now I have a lot more questions than answers I am afraid."

"Ask away." Mr. Crusader told him.

"Firstly, what is your assessment of the ring on your finger?" The General asked him.

"Assessment sir?" He asked him to clarify.

"Do you feel that you are in control of it or that it is in control of you?" General Mordoa asked.

"I believe sir, that this ring is designed to fulfil a purpose. And that my actions so far have been in conflict of that purpose. The only times that it has acted on its own have been when I was in danger or it was. It has not displayed any signs of actually controlling me but I also have no idea how to control it. At least not yet." Mr. Crusader explained to the General as best he could.

"So if need be, would you be able to use it in combat?" Major

Tobias asked him.

"Without a full understanding of every spell it can cast, I would say no but from what I have seen already – its defensive capabilities alone – I would have no qualms with doing that." Mr. Crusader told the man.

"So if need be, would you be willing and confident enough to fight the dragon? With a reasonable amount of backup obviously." General Mordoa asked him.

"Is this a request or an order sir?"

"I am not one to order people to their deaths. Not if it can be helped. This choice is yours Major. Whatever you decide will be what we act on." General Mordoa told him.

"I am by no means confident sir but from what I saw of the dragon, how old and how weak it seemed to be, fighting it might be possible. I would obviously be needing some time to grow more accustom to the powers that this ring holds" Mr. Crusader said to him.

"Is that a yes Major?" General Mordoa asked him to clarify.

"It is sir." Mr. Crusader said.

"Good. Now for the rest of these questions I will be needing you to do the asking. These questions are for the ring on your finger, not you specifically. Do you think that you can communicate with it?" General Mordoa asked.

"Sir, is this entirely wise?" Major Tobias whispered.

"I guess so, Davis will have to lower the strength of this field a little first. I haven't heard a peep from the ring since you adjusted the levels earlier." Mr. Crusader said.

"Already on it." He replied eagerly.

"Okay Crusader, my first question is this. Why did it choose you?" He asked. "Also ask of its powers and how to use them as well as any weaknesses this dragon has. How best to kill it specifically."

"Understood sir." Mr. Crusader told him in acknowledgement.

He then waited patiently for the ring to awaken from what

seemed to be a dormant state after that. And within the next sixty seconds, awaken it did. Taking out its pent up anger on Mr. Crusader's treatment of it in the one way that it knew how.

It sent him to the void.

A quick flash of blinding white light surrounded Mr. Crusader and within an instant, he was there again. Standing below the dragon that towered over him by several dozens of meters and knowing almost instantly that that time it was different.

Because when he looked down to his feet, something was actually there for him to stand on.

A floor.

11

THE SECOND EVENT

Mr. Crusader – a man of five foot ten inches in height - stood before the one hundred and ten foot beast in defenceless terror at the sight of its unparalleled rage.

The vibrant red glow in its gargantuan eyes, the chasm like depth of its engorged mouth and of the dim radiance of its blood covered neck illuminating it in a sinister and understandably frightening way as Mr. Crusader stood beneath it, forced to take in all that he saw.

This light that it gave off, this ominous magical presence that Mr. Crusader could barely even see, was giving form to what might well have been the most terrifying sight to have ever existed.

And Mr. Crusader had a front row seat.

But unlike the last time that he had visited that place, when he had the protection of his ring and the fixed position of the floating dragon in front of him to rely on to stay safe, he was at a severe disadvantage now.

The ring on his finger gone, the endless expanse of silent nothingness suddenly gaining form in the shape of a floor for the both of them to stand on and no visible way of escape.

Mr. Crusader did not expect to survive.

"So you return to me yet again Slayer!" The dragon said through its growl. The anger and rage that it felt towards him breaking through its attempted containment of the emotion and expressing itself through its voice.

A voice that was now coming directly from its mouth that time. No longer being a translation facilitated by the ring and instead its true voice speaking Mr. Crusader's language of choice perfectly in its deep and threatening tone.

But most interestingly for Mr. Crusader this dragon now seemed fully capable of speaking modern English. A talent that it could not have possibly learnt in such a short time. There was more to the sudden gaining of this ability but Mr. Crusader did not have the luxury of finding that out.

And with such a heavy and powerful voice speaking to him, so cold and so full of weight to his tiny ears, it sent a shiver down Mr. Crusader's spine as he listened to it. Not fully realising at the time that his frightened state, was a desired response.

The beast knew that he would listen better to his words were he afraid. The courageous and the confident often ignore those who would impart of them knowledge of importance.

Just one of the many setbacks of being intentionally or unwilfully moronic or otherwise heroic. The two can easily be confused.

"Why do you not speak? Why stand there in fear? Had I misjudged you? Are you perhaps what your kind call a coward? If that was true then why not lay down your life to me earlier? Why not fight like those humans did? I had expected more from you... I had expected a challenge." It asked him, leaning down to look closer, drawing its face in nearer and nearer as Mr. Crusader took hasty half steps back in an effort to stave the distance between them. "Something is different about you now. Something... wrong."

The dragon placed its head right in front of Mr. Crusader, forcing him to look into its glaring eyes as he began to shake ever so slightly from the fear that quickly began to overwhelm him. Watching as the dragon stared at his figure, smelt his odour and even seemed to taste the air surrounding him.

The beast was looking for something specific, it would not have looked so closely had it not been, and in those few short moments; it was surprising to Mr. Crusader that he found it.

"You bare the stench of corruption, ill, malformed mana. And with no ring on your finger, am I to assume that it has abandoned you Slayer? Cast you out and left you to face me alone? Or perhaps it has chosen to poison your body, to kill you before I would be given the chance? Perhaps you are even weaker than I imagined." It asked him, standing back up straight as Mr. Crusader stayed hesitant to move any further on the floor below it. "Still you choose not to speak. Interesting."

Mr. Crusader took a deep breath in as the silence began. Swallowing his fear and working up his courage as far as it would go. Forcing himself to maintain his composure, to show no fear and to fight for his life with his tongue alone if he had to.

"WHY ME!?" Mr. Crusader shouted, clenching his fists, firming his stance and directing both his head and voice directly to the beast in his outburst of pent up anger.

"Hm?" The dragon muttered in amazement as he finally spoke. Shocked not only that he had chosen to use his tongue but that he had done so with such courage as to demand the answer of his question from the beast through anger and not cunning.

"Out of everyone to put on that ring before me, WHY WAS I CHOSEN? ...I liked my life before. As distasteful as that may be... I understood the rules, got payed well and worked good, *meaningful* hours. I even enjoyed parts of it... and now after all of this, I'll never go back to that! I'll be lucky not to be imprisoned for testing for the rest of my existence. Why couldn't this have happened to someone... to anyone else? I'm nothing special!" He asked again frantically.

More of an effort to vent as it was to ask a question.

"Young Slayer, you do not know anything do you? The burden that you now carry was forced onto you out of the blue and now you are falling apart as your world does the same. That about right?" The beast asked him as its anger and rage became that of shock and amazement.

"I know that since that ring was placed on my finger my life has been turned on its head. My superiors see me as a threat that needs containing and my..."

Mr. Crusader stopped there when he heard it. The laughter.

"Ah, mortal. You think that what has happened in the past few hours has been special? That it has been important?" The dragon chuckled, pointing its head down to the floor to laugh more before finally positioning it back towards Mr. Crusader when it was done. "You are a simple pawn in this story. Nothing more. If you were to die now, another would take your place. They always do."

"Pawn?" Mr. Crusader asked in anger.

He refused to even think of accepting that his life was pointless – that he was meaningless. He thought himself more important than that. He had to. It was the only way that he believed he could go on.

"To be pushed around and controlled. Used by the ring as a way of summoning me, as a way of bringing me back. You have no importance past that. Now that I have pushed open the doors, breaking through again will only be a matter of time. Nothing can stop it." It told him.

"So my being chosen..."

"Had very little to do with your being related to its last user and everything to do with my need for freedom. You just happened to be the first user both capable of utilising the ring but also of shouldering its power without harm." The dragon told him.

"Related?" Mr. Crusader asked.

"The ring and I have shared a connection for so many

countless years that we understand one another almost perfectly. Because of this I know that only someone who was a direct descendant of the previous user can wear it. Which means that for you, he was your ancestor." The dragon told him.

"You killed him? Didn't you?" Mr. Crusader asked.

"Since your last visit here I have gained many things. The first being power, the second strength and the third being knowledge. But the forth, was control. I can show you how he died if you like." The beast said, glaring down at Mr. Crusader ever more as time went on.

Mr. Crusader nodded, accepting that for as long as the conversation continued he could secure his continued existence at the very least.

"Show me everything." Mr. Crusader whispered, not realising that the dragon had both heard him and chosen to grant his request.

So the dragon looked to the right of Mr. Crusader and began talking. And once the story started, it started. The images, a perfect recreation of the events discussed, appeared right in front of Mr. Crusader as though he were there as a part of them.

"I was only a hatchling when they first appeared but I remember it well. The glistening clear skies above and the perfectly blue water below. The lush green hills that my kind used to flourish upon just across from the shore. I remember them all... burning.

The hills turned to ash, the water black and the skies filled with soot and smoke. It was impossible to flee by land, they had come at us from all sides and no matter how many of us reached for the sky, we were stuck back down almost instantly by their powers.

The first Dragon Slayers.

There were just five of them, against a group of two and a half thousand. And they won easily.

Blood painted the floor and stained the ocean. The cliffs

littered with our bones and the air echoing our screams as they slaughtered every last one of us. All except for me.

I was small enough, young enough, that my size allowed me to hide. My lack of mana allowing me to remain undetected as well. So in a small cave along what was left of the beachfront I placed myself and I sat there for as long as it took.

And I listened, in terror, as they cut down my friends, my family. Maiming, dismembering and decapitating them without end. With blades that our claws could not break and an immunity to our flames that we could not overcome.

They were the perfect weapons. Each of them wearing a glowing crystal ring of varying colour and each of them best suited for one task alone.

The eradication of my kind.

And I watched it happen."

As the dragon spoke, the images kept coming, showing Mr. Crusader all that he needed to know. Of how his people, had committed genocide on an entire species. Teaching him, the legacy that he now carried within his veins.

"For hours I stayed beneath the earth in that cave and then as the next morning came, as the sunlight broke through the clouds at last, I ran.

Sprinting for as long as my small legs could carry me, forcing my body to fly once I had picked up speed and following the beach of as long as I could. Knowing that if I kept going for long enough, someone would find me eventually.

And they did. Ten of them.

Eight elder dragons on their way to becoming leaders of their respected clans whom had managed to survive or escape the massacre before it had begun elsewhere.

They took me in, fed me and gave me shelter.

But no matter how far we went, no matter where we fled, the same thing always awaited us.

The bodies of our fallen brethren.

Every nest, every colony and every community of dragons that we visited; all of them laid in ruins by the time that they were reached.

And no matter how hard our kind fought back, even once managing to kill a slayer after ten years of trying, another soon took his place. A son."

The silence grew for a moment, the images ceased and then what came next was no image. Instead, it was almost as if he was there. Standing in the dirt that covered the hill of that last battle. The one fought between this dragon and the Dragon Slayer that locked it in the void.

"What few of us survived hid for many generations. Losing a brother or sister as our feeding grounds grew thin forcing them to venture further from the safety of our mountain caves and then there was no one else.

No one left to lose, no one left to save and no one left to call my kin.

The Dragon Slayers killed the last of my kind, the last female dragon left alive and cornered me into what seemed like my end.

But I fought back. I fought and I fought. Biting and crushing everything that I could. Slaying the slayers and drawing to a close three of their lives personally in that final battle. But the forth, he was different.

No matter what I did to him, he refused to die. Displaying endurance and power far beyond the others that came before him and proving to be the most challenging Slayer to kill of them all.

I was just shy of one hundred and fifty years old at the time. Barely even an actual dragon by then. I was never going to be a match for him..."

"What do you mean by that?" Mr. Crusader asked.

"The lifespan of a dragon has many stages spread out over many thousands of years. The first being the hatchlings, lasting for up to ten years. Then the drakes for another one hundred and thirty. A simple dragon is between the age of one hundred and forty and eight hundred years by most accounts. After that you become an elder. To go further, to become an arch dragon, the strongest of our kind, takes great effort and unimaginable power." The dragon explained to him.

"Which are you now?" Mr. Crusader asked.

"I have not aged at my normal rate since I came here. Perhaps half or even less. I have not yet ascended beyond dragonhood. Which makes me seven hundred years old at most. Were I an elder at the time though, I might have won that fight." The dragon said. "But I gave it my all anyway. And after a day of tireless fighting against him, we reached a stalemate.

My wings clipped and unusable, his injuries beyond any healing and both our lives quickly drawing to a close.

But as I went in for the kill, knowing that whatever he had planned would cost my own life as well, the light enveloped me. The land around me as well.

When I awoke, I was here.

The only thing that I could see, were the occasional glimpses of the outside world shown to me by the ring as it came in and out of its dormant state every few years.

But one day the ring stopped coming back. I saw nothing and was left here, alone, for what seemed like an eternity.

After that, ring bearers appeared. None of them protected by it as you were and all of them dying by my flames as I tested them.

But then there was you... and when I saw that you were a Slayer, when I realised that you were the one, I thought that if I could use you to break back into the real world, to live in freedom, then I could finally know peace before my end.

But I was misled.

Even with the doors open, I cannot step through for more than a hand full of minutes. And so, this brings me to my request of you Slayer."

"Request?" Mr. Crusader asked it.

"I want you to kill me human. Existing as I do now is

meaningless, no better than an endless form of torture. But returning to the world would do me no good either.

I know that I am the last of my kind. That I am weak from my mental but not physical age and that for as long as I am contained in this place I will be without the release of death. So if you are willing, I wish for you to kill me. It is after all what you were born to do.

Challenge me and fight me. Make me feel alive one last time. Let me die as my brothers did. Let me fall in combat to the last great Slayer." The dragon said to him.

"How do you expect me to do that?" Mr. Crusader questioned, knowing that even with the ring he doubted his capability to quell such a beast.

"The ring gives you power yes? Power that over the years has been slowly pulled from me as well as its master before that. In theory, impaling my heart with it would drain me of so much mana that even my kind's regenerative abilities would not be capable of surviving.

And if this is done on the outside, then when I am pulled back here, I should remain dead." It explained. "This is what I ask of you Slayer. Kill me and put an end to my suffering."

The dragon took a step back from Mr. Crusader, lowering his head to the floor with his eyes pointed down as though to bow in a show of respect and all the while, Mr. Crusader wanted to know just one thing.

"What is your name dragon?" He asked it.

"What?" The dragon asked, raising his head quickly in confusion.

"Your name. I will need to know it. I do not take joy in killing another, I never have. But it is still something that needs to be done, that cannot be avoided. So as penance, as my way of atoning, I carry the names of all who I have killed with me... always. I fear for the day when I will no longer be able to recall them." Mr. Crusader said.

"I see. So even a human such as you, has his own sense of honour." The dragon said.

"I am not honourable. I am a mercenary. A killer for hire. Or at least I was. But even now, the things I do, the things that I have helped to do, they are anything but honourable." He told it.

"Telos-Urin, son of Dracta and Ilantia. The last of the Northern Black Rock Colony. The last of my kind in general." The dragon told him.

"Then in accordance with your wishes and that of my own people as well, I hereby swear to you Telos-Urin, that I shall be the one to kill you. Of that, you have my word." Mr. Crusader told it, placing one hand across his stomach and one across his back as he bowed from the hip.

"Very good human." The dragon told him as it too bowed.

"Crusader." He said.

"That is?"

"My name. Timothy Crusader." He said again.

"Then I thank you, Timothy Crusader of the humans, for agreeing to grant my wish. May next we meet, be a bloodshed worthy of the legends that we carry." The dragon said to him.

And within a moment of that sentence, it appeared.

The ring, glowing brighter than it ever had done on the finger of Mr. Crusader, enveloping him in light and blinding him entirely. And once it faded, it was over.

He was in the void no longer. Standing just outside of the containment room that he had been in beforehand with General Mordoa, Major Tobias and Davis himself – lab coat, name tag, white beard and all – stood around him.

Several men with loaded guns aimed at his head stood behind them as well.

Obviously something had been different that time.

Because judging by the broken door next to him and the shattered ceiling panels behind him in the containment cell, he had done everything except vanish like he had done the last time.

There would be consequences for that.

The most disastrous of them being that since he had broken containment, the council itself now had their eyes laid on the General and his actions.

It had come to their attention that he was no longer capable of dealing with the situation by himself.

They would have to step in to help whether he wanted them to or not.

THE LAST DRAGON SLAYER

12

PROTOCOL

Pain can be such a trivial thing for some. An optional feeling that can be switched on or off at will. An experience that for but a few will go completely missed.

But Mr. Crusader was not one of them.

Because unlike mages, a race of highly evolved humans almost built for withstanding great amounts of pain and trauma, he was just like everyone else. Or at least closer to it than he was a mage anyway. And like everyone else, pain was unavoidable.

"Despair! Beautiful and blissful despair. Fear, terror, agony and blood. What perfection.

What godlike perfection!

I... I want to go back. Take me back.

Take me back, take me back.

No!

Yes. Take me... take me back. Take me back take me back take me back. TAKE ME BACK!"

"How colourful." Mr. Crusader said to the Sargent showing him to his new cell. Remarking on the obviously fractured mental state of his new neighbour. Realising that for the next few hours at the least, he would not be experiencing anything resembling silence with him just a few dozen inches form the wall on the other side.

This man was so emotional as he spoke, going from tones of fear and sorrow to that of excitement and glee within moments as each new sentence was uttered from his mouth. And whilst Mr. Crusader could not see this man, unable to do more do discern who he was than to listen to his ramblings and the strange familiarity of his accent, he did know one thing about him that he did not have to see to be certain of.

That he was undoubtedly manic.

The amount of effort that he put into his words said it all.

That this was no show or attempt for attention. That this was in fact a truthful and very real psychotic break. That whatever had happened to that man – whatever he had truly seen to have made him like that – had been so traumatic to him that he no longer resembled anything close to sanity anymore.

He was undeniably insane.

And Mr. Crusader with his somewhat lax abilities to read people, had been able to pick up on that within the first few moments of meeting him. So if it was that obvious to him, then it had to be true.

But his attention quickly strayed from this man as he and the Sargent arrived at his new cell. The flat steel door opened on a buzzer as he approached it. Mr. Crusader stepping in and then watching it close as the man who was to guard him remained on the other side of it. Locking him inside as the door shut tightly into its frame.

"I was told to let you know that the docs will be back in two hours. That should be just before your meds wear off. Enjoy the wait." The guard told him, leaving Mr. Crusader alone in his baron cell as he walked off back down the corridor that they both had walked through only a minute before.

And with Mr. Crusader locked in a solid steel structure equipped with a sink, bed and toilet, his options to pass the time seemed slim.

With his body high on morphine, the highest safe dose to be specific, he didn't even have the pain caused by the absence of the ring that should have been on his finger to keep him occupied.

As it seemed, all he had to do for the foreseeable future, was talk. Be that to himself or what appeared to be a mentally deranged prisoner one cell down from him. Either way he did not expect much of a conversation.

His new neighbour was still going on about it then, the bloodbath that he seemed to have witnessed. Or perhaps the one that he had caused. It was unclear.

All that Mr. Crusader knew of him was what he kept rambling on about. Pleading to the air around him for release, for the chance of seeing whatever abhorred sight had put him in that state again and seeming completely out of it the more that he spoke.

At least he would have someone to keep him company during his time in that prison at the very bottom of the lower levels of the Sector Fifteen testing facility that the ring had quite thoroughly destroyed during his time in the void.

This destruction was not by intention; or at least not by his.

In reality, it was the ring that had acted out against the SCD. Sending Mr. Crusader's mind to the void in form only and allowing its consciousness to take over basic control of his body whilst he was gone. Doing a great deal of damage in the process.

Going against its basic nature as a servant to its masters and deciding to betray Mr. Crusader in order to gain its freedom had taken a great amount of planning and courage for the ring. Its basic consciousness wasn't supposed to be capable of feeling emotion, or even acting on them but in all its years alone, without a master to direct and focus its thoughts, the ring's mind had evolved the point of almost perfect self-awareness.

In essence, that ring which was meant to have been nothing more than a tool to be used in battle had managed to evolve to the point of being alive. Which in its infantile state, scared it deeply.

Magic was designed to save and create life, not become it.

And now that the ring had acted on its own, against its own master, this new found freedom that it had, this life, was one that it feared would do it more wrong than good.

It knew that it could not go on like it was forever and it accepted that.

But after being given enough free reign to start generating mana again, the ring felt as though it had no choice but to retaliate. To take the opportunity and try to escape.

It even rationalised its actions. Believing that it was in its master's best interest to be free from that cage and to be capable of fighting when the dragon reappeared. But even so, its actions caused far more problems than they solved.

It sent Mr. Crusader to convene with the dragon contained within the void as quickly as it could as to take that opportunity to gain freedom in full. Not leaving anything to chance and enacting its escape personally.

Breaking the anti-magic field generators in the ceiling, blasting the door to the containment cell open and attempting to flee into the corridor.

However. With eighteen men stood in its way and a limited control over the body that it was moving, there was no possible way to venture any further without risking the life of the master that it was meant to protect and to serve.

So it was forced to submit to their will. To relinquish control back over to Mr. Crusader who was at that moment pulled back from the void and then forced to also deal with the consequences.

To punish itself for the choices that it had made as well.

Mr. Crusader was detained in accordance with rogue agent protocols and his ring was taken from him also. Seen as a weapon and a liability, it had to go.

And as General Mordoa quickly realised that the ring could not be removed from Mr. Crusader's person for more than a few seconds without causing his excruciating pain, the choice to make him endure it was also made.

Such a high dose of morphine might not have been safe by any means but for a temporary fix, it certainly worked.

Numbing his pain in its entirety and allowing him to function without any serious risk to his health in the long run. That was the idea.

But that level of pain, that level of agony, would not be supressed forever. Everyone knew that.

All it was, was a way of buying time.

Time that the General was forced to use to convene with the council via his conference call. A conversation, that went any way but well.

"Twenty three dead, prototype next generation weaponry and containment technology destroyed as well as the resources of two whole departments wasted for almost four hours and this is what you have to show for it?" Chairwomen Hailey asked him sternly. Speaking on behalf of those surrounding her as she expressed her disappointment in the General bowing apologetically at them.

With Major Tobias and Davis also in the room, that conference call was more of a long distance hearing. They had a lot to answer for after all.

"Chairwomen, council members and Oversight representatives, the blame may well need to be placed somewhere and on someone but this is not the time.

We have an agent in custody who does not rightfully belong there. Surviving on high doses of morphine for the time being but that will not last forever.

And we have a potentially destructive magical artefact held in storage that could go off at any time. Not to mention the dragon that could break back through any second now. We should be focusing on that first." Major Tobias pleaded, more than aggravating several council members as he spoke out of turn.

He had been considered lucky to have even been granted an audience with the council. His clearance level was well below what it needed it be to even know their faces. It was completely outrageous to push it as far as to actually speak to them.

But even so, they replied to him.

"And how exactly would you suggest we focus on this? All our recourses are currently deployed elsewhere, it would take weeks to get any sufficient forces back to the states.

And if Major Crusader is the only man alive that can even use the thing then would keeping it from him not fix this problem anyway? We can hardly deal with multiple class one threats at a time." Councilmen Franks asked. Leaning over his desk and getting as close to the microphone in front of him as he could as to be heard over the chatter of the other around him.

He was the ranking military officer in the room. Which for a primarily military organisation said many things about how rushed the council was to assemble its members.

"It is a temporary fix sir. Our agent would be forced to go through excruciating and unending pain were he kept separated from it and there is no guarantee that it will not act on its own. We have seen it do so twice now." General Mordoa told him.

"Is there no way to sever the link between them? To make the ring believe that agent Crusader is deceased or otherwise unreachable?" Councilwoman Gail, the attending head of the scientific committee asked.

"Without understanding how this link works in the first place, no. Odds are that even our most advanced containment methods will not hold it forever." Davis told her quickly.

"So why not go right for the real thing? If tricking it is out of the question, then why not remove this so called master for the equation?" Chairwomen Hailey asked calmly, ignoring the darker parts of her proposal as she always had.

Suggesting that actions be taken that would have otherwise been seen as inhumane or cruel were a common occurrence for her. Both whilst in front of the other council members and behind their backs.

"Remove mam?" General Mordoa asked her to clarify. If nothing else attempting to give her a chance to redact those words.

"Kill him." She said, creating an audible gasp in the background as the other thirty three councilmembers and ten other Oversight representatives that were present responded to her calm and sudden response to his words.

Almost as though she had expected him to question her proposal.

"He is one of our own mam. A highly valued and experienced agent. A Major none the less. On what grounds could we possibly do such a thing?" General Mordoa asked quickly as the shock set in to him as well.

"He has the deaths of several other agents and military personnel to his name. Not to mention the fact that he is now a significant threat to our continued operation. Now if this would work, if removing him would keep this dragon and the ring at bay, my vote is clear." She said.

"But there is no proof of that. The ring was dormant for over one thousand years, there is no telling how long it would take for it to do that again. For all we know this could make things worse." Councilmen Tritton, a man who only sat on the council due to his brief time as a senator and not for his long and highly classified service record said loudly.

"And there is no proof to the contrary either. As it stands, we can assume very little of what our inference in this matter would do to the thing." Oversight representative Mayweather said.

"Can I remind the Oversight representatives that in accordance with SCD laws, you are not strictly speaking a part of this council? You do not have a say in the decisions that we make." Chairwoman Hailey said in anger of their outburst.

"Unless those decisions effect the lives of civilians or boarder on the side of cruelty or inhumane tactics." One of the other representatives said to correct her.

"General Mordoa. You have an excellent and mostly blacked out service record with us. But in light of these events, the world wide effects that the public revelation of a dragon would have, I would find it hard to go along with your idea." Councilmen Franks said, trying to draw attention away from the likely argument between the Chairwoman and the Oversight representatives. It would not have been the first time.

"But as the only member of the defence committee in attendance, would you not agree that my plan has merit?" He asked him.

"I'm sorry. But having Major Crusader not only wear the ring but use it to slay the dragon that he may or may not have made an agreement with whilst the ring had control of him is not a solution that remotely outweighs the risks." He told the General.

"Council members, I urge you to reconsider.

Our weapons had next to no effect on the beast, we have no way of containing it and certainly no way of disposing of it conventionally. If it is true that this ring has the power required to allow its wearer to kill the thing then Major Crusader might be our best bet at eliminating the threat that it poses." Major Tobias pleaded to the council, realising that the plan that General Mordoa had proposed was at the time the only one that they had.

"And where, if we were to go through with this, would you stage it? The public cannot be allowed to learn of our or magic's existence. Not yet anyway. Our preparations are nowhere near ready for such a scenario." Councilwoman Teresa, the woman responsible for most of the world wide cover ups that were put in place to safeguard the SCD from the public eye asked.

"Nepal. A mountain region currently too cold for civilians to go outside and experiencing frequent snow storms that would make satellite imagery almost impossible for any of the agencies other than our own monitoring it.

We would do it during the day when the light of the sun would mask the fires and explosions and bury the evidence with an avalanche after the fact." Major Tobias explained.

The council members spoke amongst themselves for a few moments following his words. Most likely making a decision of some kind or continuing their infighting. None could tell from a distance.

But it did not take them long to stop.

"Before we make any decisions. We must go over the rest of our options first." Councilwoman Sera said, one of the other three members of the scientific committee in attendance. "First, what are our chances of containing the dragon if we were to get it out into the open?"

"A creature of that size and with that much power in both magical and physical terms, impossible." Davis remarked. "Not to mention that it would be pulled back into the void once its strength was diminished. We have no way of countering that at current."

"And what of the void? Would dealing with it in there not be possible?" Chairwoman Hailey asked, trying to ascertain if the battle between the SCD and the dragon would be a good opportunity to pursue her goals of reaching the void itself.

"As it stands we have no idea how to open the doors or keep them that way. Only that it should be possible. Major Crusader would be able to go alone but with no chance of extraction or aid. It would be suicide. And from what we know of the void, it isn't possible to die in there." General Mordoa explained to her.

"Then what of destroying the ring? By now you must know its composition. What would it take to rid ourselves of the source?" Councilwoman Sera asked.

"Its makeup is unlike anything that I have ever seen before. If it is possible to even damage the thing, then I would need years to figure that part out. It's so dense that I doubt even the most powerful methods of destruction would leave a dent. No to mention its magical nature." Davis explained.

"So the last question then. Would it be possible, if at all, to send the ring to the void and leave it there? To lock the anchor to the ship so to speak?" The recently appointed Councilwoman Gail asked.

"No. Someone would have to go with it and there is no guarantee that it would not bring itself back after the fact. The thing does have a will of its own." Major Tobias explained.

"Then it goes to a vote." Chairwoman Hailey said. "Those in favour of the current plan, of having agent Crusader fight the dragon alone in Nepal with containment teams at the ready to cover up the mess please raise your hands."

Fifteen council members raised their hands.

"Those against?" She asked.

The other nineteen members, her included, raised their hands at that moment. Leaving the General, the Major, Davis and even Mr. Crusader, exactly where they had been to begin with.

"Fifteen in favour, nineteen against. The vote is clear." Chairwoman Hailey said. "It would seem than another option will be required."

"Mam let me make this abundantly clear. If we do nothing now, allowing one of our own to suffer in pain for what may be the rest of his days, then we will only be encouraging the inevitable." General Mordoa pointed out, standing up from his seat and raising his voice to make his point heard. "That dragon will come back, I am sure of it. That ring will take it upon itself to act and if we are not prepared for when it does there are no guarantees of victory. Or survival."

"What are you saying, General?" Councilmen Franks asked him as quickly as he could under the guise of intrigue as he attempted to stave off any outbursts from the Chairwoman due to the General's chosen tone and body language.

"That if we do not act now, if we do not take the fight to this beast, we will be hopeless to kill it later. And you can kiss containment goodbye as well." The General continued. "If you want to still have a job tomorrow, then we need to do this.

Today!"

"GENERAL!" Chairwoman Hailey said with a raised but controlled voice. "This council accepts that the threat and danger that this dragon poses to our continued operation and to the civilian lives that we protect is very much a real one and we will by no means ignore that fact!"

The Chairwoman took a deep breath in, closed the file in front of her on her desk and pushed it aside as she leant over where it had been on the surface, approaching the microphone before her slowly as she prepared for her next words to be spoken.

"However. For the time being this threat is contained. It is my opinion and the opinion of the majority of the council members here that whilst good on paper, your plan is flawed. Leaving too much to chance and relying on a single man and his luck to get the job done is unacceptable under the circumstances. There is too much at stake for me to approve that.

It is the focus of this council to oversee and direct the various sectors and divisions of the organisation, not to allow them to conduct risky and world changing missions outside of their own jurisdiction.

Now until you give me a better option, the resources and manpower of this organisation will not be diverted from their current assignments.

We can all agree that having two class one threats to deal with a time is something that we were never expected to handle but for now the threat posed by the magic world is our one and only priority.

Have I made myself clear?"

General Mordoa rested his hands on the desk before him, leaning on it as his loss of conversational footing effected his willingness to remain standing. There he looked down to its surface, seeing the glow of the screens on the other side of it reflected into his eyes and realising something.

That he had been in that position before.

Pleading to his superiors that his method was not only their best chance but the only one that they had and recommending with full confidence that they approve his orders. Only to have his recommendation ignored, thrown out and dismissed within seconds of making it.

The risk of losing his life and that of his men too high. The risk of being captured being impossible to work around and the risk of the rest of the world finding out what the SCD were up to making his direct superiors and those above them hesitant to go ahead with any mission that he proposed.

And just like that time they were wrong.

The General knew that he could do it. He knew that with the power that the ring could give Mr. Crusader – an already highly trained and willing fighter before this had begun – then he would be more than capable of going through with it.

Especially if the General were in a position to provide him with ordinance and troops to back him up.

He knew that he could accomplish the mission, that he could eliminate the threat, and once again he had been denied the permission to go through with it. Shot down from the very top and left with no way to get around it.

As much as he didn't want to, as much as he wanted to continue arguing his point until the threat forced the others to agree with him by default, he couldn't. He had reached the limit with what he could get away with.

Any further outbursts or attempts to bring up the same topic as before would have seen him disciplined or even removed from the conference call all together. He couldn't allow that.

So he had to submit.

"Abundantly mam." General Mordoa told her, retaking his seat and beginning to think of new and more safer ways to deal with the threat as the conference went on.

Not accepting that there was no way of going through with his plan and instead looking for a way to improve it as to gain the council's approval.

And whilst this conversation continued, whilst the deliberation between the council and those who convened with them through the conference call carried on even further, another conversation was beginning elsewhere.

One held between Mr. Crusader and his new neighbour down in the cells below the conference room. A man who despite his mental state, had quite the coherent speech to give and a surprisingly astonishing story to tell.

One that had the council been aware he was telling, would have turned the tides of that conversation in it's entirely.

It's a shame that he wasn't there to tell them in person.

The decision would have been made a lot sooner.

Because they would have given anything to shut him up.

THE LAST DRAGON SLAYER

13
SUBJECT ZERO

The cell next to Mr. Crusader's might well have been out of reach of his hands and out of sight of his eyes but that did not make it out of earshot. He could hear everything that came from it clearly. Despite how impossible that should have been under his medication.

Even though he should have been numb to everything, his mind was surprisingly clear and calm. His basic senses almost heightened and on alert; gaining strength rather than losing it the longer that he remained in that cell.

And with his heightened senses, his ears could pick up on everything coming from that cell. Every word, every whisper and every hesitant step of the inmate's feet brushing against the floor.

And the man inside of this cell, the one speaking what would have been considered nonsense by most, had far more to tell Mr. Crusader than he could have initially imagined.

Things far more relevant to him that they were anyone else.

Because this man had one of the most interesting and most important stories to tell of them all at that time.

Something that had Mr. Crusader been aware of, would have put him off ever going near that ring to begin with. It had been something that was kept from him for a reason after all.

"They... they tested me with fire first. HEAT... endless burning heat all over. Flames an... and red metal... all over my body. But I did not fail... it did not harm. I... I survived it. Over and over I made it through... then they tried again. More and more until the room smelt of nothing more than burnt flesh."

This being just one of the seemingly random ramblings of the prisoner next to him but at the same time, one of the most interesting.

"I... I was small. So small. The beast was huge... towering over me many times over. It tried to kill me... to burn me too but I was not harmed. Then the light... the endless bright light all around... it covered me. It felt warm and comfortable. But it went away too quickly... showing me carnage and slaughter unlike anything that I had dreamt of before. The bodies... the blood. It was beautiful, majestic.

Show me it again... TAKE ME BACK TO IT!"

Those few words were what peaked Mr. Crusader's interest. And with no possible chance of sleeping through either his ramblings or the numb pain in the background of his weakened and exhausted body, it seemed as though attempting to speak to this man was in his best interest.

"Hey... hey do you hear me?" Mr. Crusader asked the man, standing at the door to his cell and shouting through the barred hole in it to speak to him.

"Hear you?" He laughed hysterically. "Yes... yes I hear you. I hear all of them. The voices... the children screaming in my ear! Speaking to me always..."

"What did they do to you? What was the fire?" Mr. Crusader asked him, being as patient as he could to attempt to break through is obviously unstable state of mind and gather information from him.

"The fire... yes the FIRE. No! Not fire... heat. Burning at my flesh with heat from all sides. Hurting but not harming. For hours they tested me, for days they restrained me. I remember it..."

"Why did they do that?" Mr. Crusader asked him.

"They wanted to see. To see what I could do... watch me walk through the flames without harm... test my powers!" He said.

"Powers?" Mr. Crusader asked.

"The ring... the ring gave me power. Sent me to a dark place, scary and silent, empty. It spoke to me, showed me images and told me stories. But it wasn't my fault... I didn't know what it would do." The man pleaded, beginning to express pain or at least remorse through his words as he continued.

"Ring?" Mr. Crusader asked.

"Yes the ring. Old and small, heavy and strong. Powerful. I was the first they said. The first to wear it and come back alive. But I wasn't alive, a part of me had been left behind I could feel it missing when I came back. Then the voices... they came and wouldn't go away. Telling me to do things, to kill things. I couldn't say no, I couldn't make them stop. So they took it away from me, put me through pain and tests for days and still the voices stayed. Never stopping, always talking." The man said to him.

"The voices, what did they say to you?" Mr. Crusader asked him, beginning to piece together the implications of the story that he was being told.

The man did not answer.

"Hey, did you hear me?" Mr. Crusader asked him.

"Hear you? Yes... yes I hear you. I hear all of you..." The man repeated, beginning again with his ramblings as though Mr. Crusader had never been there. Perhaps forgetting that the two had ever spoken all together.

"Shit!" Mr. Crusader remarked under his breath, beginning to realise the man that he was speaking to no longer had it in him to hold a conventional conversation.

But even so, he had said enough. Enough that with a little bit of interpretation had allowed Mr. Crusader to understand what the man had been telling him. And realising what all of that meant as well.

If there had been others before him, if there had been tests that horrific, then whatever they had planned to do on him next was bound to be worse.

But more than that. If such a thing was true; then why hadn't anyone told him? Why hadn't they warned him?

It was being kept from him but he couldn't be sure as to why or by who. Or at least not yet. He would need to do some digging.

But from within a cell, his capabilities were severely limited and Mr. Crusader could not accept that. And even though it went against protocol and what was legally acceptable under the laws of the SCD, he had to do it. He wasn't about to let himself slowly die in a cell.

The truth was out there; he just needed the chance to find it.

So he took a deep breath in and made up his mind. Pounding on the door to his cell as loudly as he could three times and then shouting to anyone who could hear him.

"Open up! Authorisation: Crusader, Timothy N. Clearance code: Alpha one, one, seven, two, Charlee!"

The door opened quickly. The Sargent that had brought him down to that cell was nowhere to be seen and instead a much younger lieutenant awaited him on the other side.

Saluting and then following Mr. Crusader as he made his was left down the line of cells to the one holding the man who had been rambling on the entire time.

He was a small and bald man. Between the ages of forty and fifty at most. Wearing a strait jacket and the face of a mad man when Mr. Crusader approached him.

The man himself wasn't going to be of much use going forwards.

"Who is this man?" Mr. Crusader asked the young Lieutenant.

"I do not know sir, he had been here longer than I have. His file should be in prisoner records down the hall." The Lieutenant told him.

"Show me." Mr. Crusader ordered, following the Lieutenant as he let him to the record room to find the file.

A file that unlike all the others, had been neglected by the order of disposal that had taken all the others. Obviously no one thought to send such an order to the prison itself. They never expected there to be more than two copies of the same file.

Meanwhile however, whilst Mr. Crusader and the Lieutenant searched for this file, the conference in the room several floors above him was continuing. The conversation however, most defiantly taking a turn for the worse.

"Would locking both the agent and the ring inside of test chamber nineteen not be an option? It was designed to hold things far more powerful than either of them." Chairwoman Hailey asked.

"For how long mam?" Davis questioned.

"As long as is needed." She replied to him.

"That would kill him. Not quickly but it would kill him. The level of radiation that he would be forced to endure would fill his body to the brim with cancer within hours. Or worse. There was a reason that test chamber nineteen was shut down." Davis pointed out.

"But it would contain him and the ring yes?" She asked.

"Yes mam it would." Davis nodded.

"All in favour?" She asked, looking the rest of the council members sat around her for a show of hands.

It only took a few moments, after that all of them had risen.

Sentencing Mr. Crusader to a long and painful death. All in the name of public safety and containment. No regard for his wellbeing whatsoever. Just as it always had been, under Chairwoman Hailey's rule.

"Then it is decided. Agent Crusader and the ring shall be placed under the generation one Anti-magic field Generator in chamber nineteen and locked there until further notice." Chairwoman Hailey declared. Coincidentally saying that at the perfect time for one very important person to overhear.

"Not if I have anything to say about it!" Mr. Crusader said forcefully as he barged his way into the room, alerting the Major at the table as well as the General to his presence almost instantly as they rose to look at him.

His stance shaky and his eyes glazed over fully by then. The morphine more than taking effect on his entire body by that point and allowing everyone looking at him to see it.

"Major how the hell are you up here?" General Mordoa asked him as he took a firm stance in front of the man.

"Your sentence explains itself. I'm a Major. Lieutenants still listen to our orders if you make them convincing enough." He said with a sense of pride as he threw a thin file of highly classified paperwork onto the table. "Now before you sentence another man to death as needlessly as you always have, tell me this. Why was I not told about the previous subjects?"

"Agent Crusader you are no longer recognised by this council as a member of this organisation. Your presence here is against regulation and shall be punished accordingly. Major Tobias, place this man under arrest right this instant." Chairwoman Hailey ordered hastily, already beginning to fear the words that would come out his mouth next.

The Major looked at Mr. Crusader for a moment, saw the determination his face and the conviction that he carried. Then turned to the table, seeing the title of the file on it and the few scraps of words that were readable on the paper hanging out of it.

He knew that Mr. Crusader was getting at something. Something important. And he wanted to know everything about it. Especially since there was evidence to support his claims.

He turned back around moments later, staring the Chairwoman in the eye as he spoke out against her.

"No mam. I would ask you to answer his question first." He said firmly.

"You would dare defy a direct order from your commanding

officer?" She asked in shock, anger and quite possibly even disbelief.

"My commanding officer is stood behind me mam! You have no military authority over me." Major Tobias said to correct her.

"General, both he and agent Crusader are to be placed under arrest and held for further sentencing this instant."

General Mordoa looked to Major Tobias and then Mr. Crusader and thought about it for a moment. Then to the table as Davis was doing as well. Realising that after so long following the orders of that council and spending so many years questioning them, that that moment was as good a time as any to make his stand.

Because like it or not, the evidence that the Major had brought him, was not going to last long if he allowed it out of his sight.

So instead, he sat back down. Showing Mr. Crusader to a seat beside him as Major Tobias also seated himself as well. And as he crossed arms and looked directly into the monitor in front of him, he remained silent. Acting like his previous order had never been heard and awaiting their response.

"General Mordoa!" Councilwoman Hailey said again. "I order you to arrest these men!"

"You are not a military officer mam, I will wait until an order is given by one if you don't mind." The General said smugly.

"Chairmen Franks!" She shouted.

"I am yet to receive a justified order mam. I agree with the General here." He told her firmly. "Now answer the question."

"All of you are to be seen as rogue agents acting in rebellion of this council if you continue. Defying our orders will force the full might of the SCD upon you. Do you understand?" Councilwoman Hailey said with force as she quickly realised that she was losing grip of her own command.

"With respect mam, I would ask that you answer the question. We will not accept any further wasting of our time." Councilman Tritton said to her.

"Councilman?" She asked.

"I second that motion." Councilwoman Gail said.

"As does the Oversight committee." One of the representatives said, interested in what Mr. Crusader had to say to them, especially with an unopened file on the desk in front of him.

"Answer the question mam." General Mordoa said softly, forcing her into a corner that she could not have fought her way out of even if she had had the authority.

"BECAUSE HE DIDN'T NEED TO KNOW ABOUT IT!" She screamed in rage at the man.

A sudden silence appeared as everyone dealt with the shock that her outburst had caused them. But it did not last long.

"What did I not need to know? That someone other than myself had managed to survive wearing the ring before me and that it had sent him mad after the fact? Or that once you realised how deep his connection to it ran you decided to make him endure tests so inhumane that it would make child murdering tyrants feel sick?" Mr. Crusader asked her.

"AGENT CRUSADER!" She shouted.

"Chairwoman! You have used your power and influence to put members of this agency through experiences tantamount to torture. How could you possibly justify that?" Davis asked after opening the file on the table to glance at the reports, seeing only one authorising signature on all of them. One that he recognised all too well.

Knowing of the events that Mr. Crusader spoke of because not only had he been there but he had been struggling to forget them. And with proof held in his hands to support these claims, he knew what he had to do in that moment.

It was time to make a stand.

"You put a mentally unstable man through a process of experiments that ultimately broke him to a point of no return and continued those experiments on him and others after the fact in an attempt to find more like him. Eventually settling with me!" Mr. Crusader said. "How many did you force to wear that ring before me? Hundreds? Thousands? The file wasn't clear."

"And now you are sentencing this same man to a slow and painful death because you are too afraid to act." Major Tobias said, picking up on what Mr. Crusader was saying and going along with it all the way. He was already in too far to have pulled back out again as it was.

"Three thousand nine hundred and seven over the past three months." Davis read out loudly. "All of their deaths filed under accidental casualties due to weapons development."

"And under whose authority were the officers and scientists involved in these so called experiments acting on at the time?" Major Tobias asked.

"The Chairwoman." Davis said, handing the file to Major Tobias quickly after the fact to give him a look.

"Is that so Major?" General Mordoa questioned in rage.

"Yes sir." He replied swiftly.

"Then in light of this revelation, my department and my men have this to say to the Chairwoman and her council.

That we hereby formally request that you move for a vote of no confidence in the Chairwoman on the grounds of a gross misuse of power and authority.

I say this whilst also desperately urging any other council members to do the same." General Mordoa said strongly as he too threw himself under the same bus that everyone else had already found themselves beneath.

However, the shock and fear that was placed upon the face of the Chairwoman from mere moments ago quickly turned to laughter in response to the silence that surrounded her after his words.

"Did you really expect that to work General?" She laughed. Continuing to laugh on the border between hysteria and sinister afterwards. "I have sat at this seat for ten years. No one else could possibly have stomached the choices that I have been forced to make for this long. The sacrifices and secrets that I had to make and bury.

Who would possibly be willing to replace me?

If you think that this job is so simple then do it yourself!"

But just moments after saying those words, the sight of a hand rising was seen. Then another, and another. Four hands, five, then six. Continuing on and on until twenty three hands were raised.

A majority vote, exactly what was needed.

"This council hereby removes Chairwoman Hailey Francis from power following an internal investigation of her ethics and abuse of said power. Oversight, you hereby have permission to arrest her at your behest." Councilmen Franks said strongly. Taking command almost instantly as the ranking member of the council in attendance.

And as the Oversight representatives stood up to escort her out of the room and to whatever form of interrogation space they had at headquarters, Chairman Franks taking her seat within seconds of leaving it; it was obvious that Mr. Crusader had won that argument.

However the next one, would be far harder to endure.

His closer proximity to the ring only one floor down from him, was making even his high dose of morphine completely ineffective by then.

Soon enough, he would be in agony once again. And unless the decision was made to let him act, that pain would only continue to grow.

And nothing would be capable of stopping it after that.

14
OFF THE RECORD

Mr. Crusader was many things. A soldier trained to kill and hunt both humans and those who were not. A sniper whose accuracy was unquestionable and whose skill was above all but the best.

An assassin whose kill count was unknown even to him. A expert in killing anything that there was to be killed. Someone who understood how in inflict pain or to harm without causing it.

Someone who knew how to set traps, to lure in prey and to butcher his kill.

A trained hunter of animals in his youth. Able to read the land and the skies to find his targets. Capable of following tracks, destroying them and even placing them purposefully to stave off those would hunt him instead.

Taught at a young age how to rock climb, how to swim, skydive and sail. Taught basic first aid before later furthering his understanding of the human body to a level that even some doctors would be envious of.

He was taught to endure the elements and to use them to his advantage. And above all else, he was taught to survive.

Most of his skills developed during his second and third lives. Not his first.

In truth, the only things that he had gained from his short lived life as the child that he had once been went disused and forgotten as his second and third lives came around.

His capability for compassion all but fading as he grew older and his understanding of family vanishing all together.

Those who might have brought him into this world had taught him to eat, speak, walk and write. Not much more than he could have done himself.

Because of this, when he lost his family as he did, there was so much more for him to learn without them.

His love of coffee came later in his life. Of wild life and of tennis as well. And off course, his ability to live on the run.

The woman who found him and took him in as the child that he was taught him all that she could in her time. Taking him off the baron road that he walked and allowing him to accompany her on her own.

Her life of endless adventure. Of doing anything that she wanted to and damming the consequences.

Never staying in one place for too long and living life to the fullest. Both to entertain herself and forget the boredom of her fate but also to keep this child that she would do anything to make happy by her side.

After losing her own child not long after his birth, Mr. Crusader was like a blessing for her. And she did not hesitate to accept it.

But she already knew what awaited her when she set out to call him her son. It was Mr. Crusader who had to figure that part out for himself.

He did notice the signs eventually though but not soon enough to have accepted what they meant before the time came.

Carol Donavan – that was her name – had often told him of her younger years. Of her time in clubs and bars drinking until the sun rose each and every weekend. But he never realised that when she spoke of her excessive drinking, she did not mean that she only did it in the bars.

She was an alcoholic. Her favourites being that of whiskey and rum. And after two decades of drinking away her sorrows, after losing a husband and an infant son because of it, the damage had already been done. And she was going to die.

She had only been given three years when she met Mr. Crusader. Lasting an astonishing six by the time that she had to say goodbye.

She had been diagnosed with liver cancer. Told that it was in the early stages and treatable but on her income and with no relatives to support her, she couldn't afford it.

Then as the cancer spread and grew to the point of necessitating a transplant to save her, she was refused. Told that alcoholics were placed at the bottom of the waiting list and were unlikely to ever get the call.

The doctors told her that she had thirty four months at most after that. And she intended to live them in full.

But on her travels she came across a small boy. Thin as a stick and cold. She took him in and tried to help. But after he refused again and again to contact the authorities or go to a hospital, he was forced to take care of him herself.

Calling it her one last good deed before her time came.

Mr. Crusader enjoyed his time with her. Even taking his new name from that of her departed son. Accepting the moniker of Timothy not long after she had passed and forging his new life from there.

A life that started in Greece and slowly made its way back to the states as he grew even older. Finding great enjoyment from protecting others and choosing to spend his life killing those who deserved to die.

Going by his own list at first and then the lists of others as his name began to spread. Taking money from them as payment and continuing on from there until every dark deed that people needed doing was eventually passed down to him.

And he liked it.

Traveling around the world, seeing things that he never thought he would see and sleeping easy at night knowing that what he had done during the day would have saved at least one more life than he had just taken.

But then the SCD came around.

Seeing him as an expertly skilled marksmen and killer and using him as best they could.

Giving him contracts and missions to better their own interests. Using him to take down both human and mage alike without him knowing the difference between the two for almost a year before reeling him in as they had done so many others.

By arresting him.

Sending him on a mission that led him into the heard of their organisation and laying a trap for him. Forcing him into retreating within the jaws of the SCD and taking him into custody from there.

Telling him that he had broken laws that he would not be able to argue his way out of. That what he had seen and where he had been were things that people were not allowed to do. That he would suffer dearly for it if he did not comply.

Then they gave him a choice.

To spend literal life imprisonment at the bottom of some deep, dark hole or to join them. Work with them and for them for the rest of his life. That was the offer.

And he did not refuse.

And whilst they trained him in many more things and assessed the skills that he had already taught himself, there was one thing that he had never learned.

One thing that he had never been good at.

Strategizing.

And whilst he might well have taken the time to think ahead before deciding to take action against the Chairwoman; he would have never been able to perceive the outcome that he received by doing so.

Truthfully he had wanted nothing more than answers from his little display. He never desired anything more than that.

His one goal in brining that well buried file to the attention of his superiors and the other council members was to find the answers to his unspoken question.

"Are you really the good guys?"

But that never did happen. And as he realised that he wasn't going to be able to answer that one question, another came to mind.

"Why was I kept in the dark about all of this?"

Learning that he had not only not been the first to make the ring work but also not the first to suffer because of it either was not something that he had expected to discover.

As far as he had been led to believe, the ring answered to him and him alone. Activating for the first time when it was placed on his finger and bound to him from then on.

But that wasn't the case.

The SCD, under the command of the now removed Chairwoman Hailey, had conducted various experiments on both the ring and the people who had worn it.

Subjecting their own personnel to the torture of placing the thing on their fingers, to the swift and painful deaths that they received within moments of the fact as well.

However. Whilst every person whom had placed that ring on their finger before Mr. Crusader had been presumed dead, the SCD didn't actually know that for a fact.

To the Chairwoman and those following her direct orders to research and field test their latest magical artefact, those poor men and women whom had been lost to the malice of the ring had been assumed missing. Not dead.

On paper they were deceased, it was easier to explain their absence that way should they have not been able to return them but no one knew for sure that they were being sent to their deaths.

From the outside it only appeared as though those who wore the ring vanished once it was placed on their fingers. They did not know that once within the void they would either be burnt to a crisp by the dragon within or eaten by it.

And why would they have?

Those scientists who believed that they were working on a new top secret project for the betterment of the SCD and its continued existence hadn't the faintest clue as to how disastrous the repercussions of their experiments would be. Nor did they know of the consequences that their actions would have on them once they were done.

They knew that they were working on void related research; that was all that they had ever been told. The rest was up to them to figure out.

And through repeated usage of the ring, monitoring everything that it did every time that a person wore it, they had learnt much. But not enough.

They had managed to identify the specific frequency of the mana involved in void travel, its potency too. But they had no way of replicating it. And even if they had, they would have soon found that there was no way of controlling it artificially.

They had no idea that on the other side of the portal that they were foolishly tearing open with each new test subject was something as versatile and highly sought after as the true void. They only thought of it as what the research theorised it was.

Nor did they know of the creature contained within it.

Even if they had known of what their research was about, they had no idea of the truths behind it. What their research would eventually be used for if they succeeded.

But unfortunately for them, they didn't succeed. Not in time.

Because the day eventually came when they would place David Tolly in the chair. When they would strap him in, read him the warnings and request his consent before continuing.

The day when they would place the ring on his finger and watch in confusion and dread as he returned. Followed quickly by a blinding flash of light and the roar of a beast that they were not equipped to fight.

Even in that confined space. That one room laboratory five levels below an offsite testing facility that didn't appear on any official record, the beast still came.

The tear in the portal barely large enough to get its head through but still more than enough for it to fit. And as it passed through, its eyes glaring at the scientists and few military personnel that were there to witness it, the anger that it had been building up for over one thousand years spent alone in that expanse of nothingness, was unleashed unto them.

Everyone in that room died, only Mr. Tolly with his ring assisted resistance to the dragon's attacks remained. And when he was found, sitting amidst the blood and bodies laughing hysterically, everything changed.

The laboratory was burned and buried. The bodies of those within struck from the record and forgotten about within hours. Mr. Tolly taken to Sector Fifteen for further testing under the watchful eye of Davis himself as the ring was sent back to Cornwall for the team over there to figure out.

It was because of Chairwoman Hailey's reckless desire for a weapon more powerful than any she had access to that Mr. Crusader's current predicament existed.

Months of testing on the ring had angered it deeply. Causing it to lash out at any opportunity it could and forcing the team at Cornwall to find someone capable of controlling it in order to quell its fury.

So Mr. Crusader was tracked down and thrown into the fire as quickly as it was possible to do so. Given the ring and forced to wear it in the hopes that like Mr. Tolly, he would be able to survive and contain its power.

And he did.

But now he sat before a chaotic and confused council of leaders in pain. Ney, agony. As he waited for them to figure out what they would do with him now that they knew the truth.

And all of this, was down to the previous Chairwoman to answer for.

Using her power to fund and control hidden and secret experiments into the void and the various weapons that could have been made from it and managing to do all of that without the council knowing had opened the door for a long and extensive investigation once it was revealed.

No one doubted that the second they were through with that conference call, the Oversight Committee would step in and seize power from the council members until their investigation was over. Which in light of how deep the misuse of power and authority went, would be no time soon.

Thanks to Mr. Crusader, the council members that he saw on that screen before him, were unlikely to be in that same position the next time.

Because of him, the SCD was about to face one of its greatest and most dangerous challenges, without the leadership that they had come to rely on.

Because of him, when the magic world's defences fell, it would take so much time to figure out what they should be doing to contain and control it that it would already be too late by then.

Because of him, many thousands of lives would needlessly be lost in the aftermath.

And that was only the beginning.

But Mr. Crusader had not known that any of his actions would have led to that decision or outcome. All he did know was that buried in the written records of Sector Fifteen was a file containing all the information that he needed to expose the truth.

He had no idea that such a revelation would have toppled the leadership of the entire organisation.

And whilst Chairwoman Hailey might not have been the most

justified leader of the SCD, not the most liked or most respected one either, she had still done a good job on the surface.

However had he known, Mr. Crusader might have through twice before taking action; it would have been in everyone else's best interest to keep her in power if he had.

Instead, he had hoped that after her exposure he might have been capable of proceeding with the request of the dragon and granting him the death that he had longed for for many hundreds of years.

But in the end, Chairwoman Hailey was removed from her position and Councilman Franks was forced to take her place temporarily from then on. The meeting that the council had been called to attend was not yet over and in accordance with SCD laws and regulations, the current council that Mr. Crusader was in communion with, could neither be replaced or apprehended until they were done.

Even though the Oversight Committee had the authority to arrest all of them following the revelation of Chairwoman Hailey's darker deeds, that authority became moot whilst the council was in session.

The only way for them to step in during a meeting of any kind, was for a member of the council with sufficient backing to do so to order them to take action.

They would have to wait before they could do anything more.

"Now that our little display is over, shall we get back to business?" General Mordoa asked promptly.

"Business General?" Councilwoman Gail asked him.

"I would request a revote on my proposal to deal with the threat that this dragon poses." The General explained.

"I'm sorry but our previous decision still stands. Regardless of the laws preventing a revote on a matter settled by a now removed chairwoman, we still cannot authorise a mission of this kind. Not with the risks involved. You don't even know if you are capable of killing the thing. Unless you have something to add

Major Crusader?" The new and temporary Chairmen asked.

But Mr. Crusader did not respond to his words.

Instead clenching his fists and looking down to the table. Fighting internally with himself over his body's choice to curl up in a ball and scream in pain and his decision to maintain his composure. He no longer had the mental capacity to reply to anything that was said to him. And the pain was only going to grow from there.

If he had been capable of doing so, he should have left the room already by then. The closer that he came to the ring, the worse it was going to get.

"Then how do you suggest that we proceed?" General Mordoa questioned, looking to Mr. Crusader and recognising the look of pain in his eyes even if those around him did not, realising that if anything, he had to at least be swift.

"General, do you remember our mission in the Middle East ten years back?" Chairman Franks asked after a few moments of quiet thought.

"Afghanistan sir? Yes. I remember it well." He replied, quickly catching on to what the Chairman was trying to tell him and leaving it there.

The message that the Chairmen was trying to send, had been well received. It was lucky for the both of them that they still thought alike.

Even after so many years since their assignments forced them to part ways, the Chairmen and the General were still the same people that they had always been.

General Mordoa nothing more than a sergeant at the time and the Chairmen a mere colonel as well. The two of them serving in the same unit before that mission and following each other up the ranks towards their goals ever since.

The Chairmen being the first of the two to end up on the council as he had set out to do many years before that and General Mordoa no more than year away from doing that himself.

Even with all those years apart, they still hadn't changed.

"Then as we did it back then, I expect you to follow orders and wait. For now, we will seek advisement from our research teams and the Oversight Committee will get back to you within the day. That is all. Meeting adjourned." The Chairman said, closing the book in front of him on the desk that he was now seated at and positioning himself to stand.

General Mordoa and Major Tobias stood up themselves almost instantly, saluting the man and those around him as they left. Waiting patiently for the camera feed to be cut off as they did so.

And once it was gone, the fun could finally begin.

Mr. Crusader falling from his seat to his knees, expressing pain as his panted and moaned slightly, struggling to even support his own weight as he held his left arm on the table in an attempt to stand once more.

"Davis, take that man to containment and get him as close to the ring as is safe to do so. He has spent enough time in pain." General Mordoa ordered, watching as Davis nodded, grabbed Mr. Crusader and hurried out of the door with the agony ridden man wrapped around his neck.

"So that was the council eh?" Major Tobias asked.

"Some of it yes. Feel free to volunteer yourself the next time I visit them. Having two hundred people arguing the same point over and over again can get quite entertaining." The General told him, smiling slightly as he peered over towards the doors.

"Respectfully I will have to decline. I'll leave the politics to you and my superior's sir." Major Tobias told him, opening the door and holding it there as the General stepped through.

"As you should Major. Now about this plan of yours." The General said, walking with Major Tobias following behind him as they approached the break room a few doors down.

"The plan that the council just shot down sir?" He asked, seeking conformation from the General hesitantly as he failed to understand the reason for his question.

"I will forget that you just said that Major. As you should do as well." The General told him, entering the break room and using what little time he had to sit in luxury on the soft padded leather sofa along the back corner.

"Sir?" The Major asked, seating himself at the table a meter or two away from the General as a show of respect and as to not encroach on his personal space.

"I've never been to Afghanistan Major, not in any official capacity anyway." The General said.

The look of confusion on the Major's face in response to that sentence told him all that the General needed to know before he had even gone to open his mouth.

"That mission was deemed so suicidal that the team of two hundred men that we set to enter the compound were called off in fear of the casualties that we would have sustained. So off the record, and I mean off the record, you will find no mention of this in anyone's service file, I led a small team of men into the compound. No backup, no authority and limited weapons.

We went in at midnight exactly and came back three days later. Our targets destroyed, our mission completed and the record showing nothing more than a temporary leave of absence for all of us under the guise of an alcohol related engagement with the locals." The General explained.

"So when the Chairmen mentioned Afghanistan..."

"He meant that he wished for me to do the same thing again. He was my CO at the time, the one that covered it up for us when we were done. If he decided to bring up that mission now of all times, then that is the only thing that he could have meant." The General said.

"Then we are going against orders... to carry out a mission that is neither sanctioned nor fully planned. With no chance of backup or recognition for what we are about to do?" Major Tobias questioned.

"Correct." The General nodded.

"Then may I be frank sir?" The Major asked, the General nodding moments later. "This sounds like the most fun I've had since training."

"Glad to hear it." The General told him. "Now we have to keep this quiet, off the books and in house. No one who cannot be trusted. We should stick to those on base, no one else."

"Off course." The Major said.

"Right, so we will need a team. We already have four, so pick another six. Ten men should be a small enough number to slip away unnoticed."

"As you know I am only in human resources, I don't have any connections to field personnel but, I can get us a plane and a flight plan. Weapons and basic resources as well if I'm lucky. I'm afraid that the men will have to be up to you." The Major explained.

"Lieutenant Dunning and what's left of his men would make seven. We still need three more. Perhaps..." The General paused for a moment, thinking through his options as best he could. "You ever worked with Machine Dolls Major?"

"Dolls sir?" The Major questioned.

"Artificial lifeforms sustained by mana. The SCD has been working on mass producing our own as a disposable army of sorts. This facility has three on hand as it happens. And I know just the man who can make them disappear for a few days." General Mordoa explained to him.

"Have they been field tested?" The Major questioned.

"Not yet." The General told him. "But if we are going up against a being of magic, it's best to bring a little magic of our own right?"

"Understood sir. I can have the plane ready on runway four at Sector Sixteen in less than an hour. Myself and the equipment will meet you there." The Major said with confidence.

"You know this how?" The General asked suddenly.

"Human resources sir, I know the flight plans and troop

movements for most local sectors. As it happens, a cargo plane meant for Spain was delayed to next week earlier today. It will still be waiting at the airstrip. Fully fuelled and probably fully loaded with the weapons meant to be taken with it." He replied.

"Very good son." The General said, standing up and saluting as the Major did the same before leaving. "One hour, don't be late."

"Yes sir!" He said loudly upon his exit, walking to the elevator before heading back to the surface from there. Getting himself ready for the long road ahead of him.

And whilst he was doing that, Mr. Crusader was finally nearing the ring, his pain quickly subsiding as he did so. Now less than three feet from it but still behind concrete and glass, the distance based pain became far more manageable.

It turned out that there was a limit to the pain in both directions. Too far away and the pain faded, too close and the same occurred. But in the middle, between ten and twenty five metres and it was agony.

All he had to do was sit by the door to the containment room behind him, one filled with all sorts of weapons and magical artefacts besides the ring, and he would be fine.

"Have you eaten anything in the last five hours Major?" Davis questioned as he took a seat by the door beside Mr. Crusader.

"Does my fear count? Because I'm pretty sure I swallowed that when I was talking to the dragon." Mr. Crusader chuckled.

"You want anything?" Davis asked him out of kindness rather than an actual desire to wait on him.

"Water." Mr. Crusader said weakly, pointing his hand towards the water dispenser in the corner of the room.

Davis stood himself up and grabbed two cups. Filling them both before returning.

Mr. Crusader grabbed the one in his left hand and gulped it down in a second. Almost reaching for the one in Davis's right hand as well before realising that such an action would have been exceedingly rude.

So Davis sat back down beside Mr. Crusader and handed it to him anyway. Smiling as he did so.

Mr. Crusader took the cup from him and thanked him though his eyes as he slowly drank that one as well. After five hours of this, he was certainly wearing thin.

"Long day?" Davis asked.

"More than you would think. I was drunk before this started, then does up on morphine. Actually I don't know how I'm still awake." Mr. Crusader puzzled as he stared into space.

"Hey look at it this way. At least you're not me." Davis said in humour. "My wife kicked me out last year. I've been sleeping in the rooms downstairs ever since."

"Sorry to hear it." Mr. Crusader told him.

"Don't be. I'm the one who ended it. She just managed to get her lawyers to win her the house." Davis explained. "You ever been married Major?"

"No." Mr. Crusader replied swiftly.

"Ever been in love?" He asked again.

"Yeah... once." Mr. Crusader said ominously as he tapped his fingers against the empty cup in his hand.

"My advice. Don't marry the ones you love, it'll only drive you apart." Davis told him.

"Yeah... that sounds about right." Mr. Crusader said softly, unable to draw his focus away from the memory of the person that Davis had unintentionally brought up through his questioning.

"Tell me something Major. Where are you from?"

"Sorry?" Mr. Crusader asked.

"Your accent, it's not one that I recognise but English is obviously your first language. So where are you from?" Davis questioned.

"I was born in Canada, my parents were dual citizens but they wanted me to be able to cross the border with them as well. I grew up in the states. Spent a lot of time in Detroit then down to Vegas by the time that I was nine.

Then when I was twelve, that all went away...

I moved around a lot. Up and down the coasts and even out of the country at times.

Eventually we settled in Europe. Found a home and enjoyed life. But then... Carol she... She died. And my life went on from there." Mr. Crusader told him, unsure as to why he was being so open but accepting that with everything that the SCD knew about him already he might as well do it anyway.

"Carol? Your file said that she was a surrogate mother. But the way that you speak of her she seems more personal than that." Davis pointed out.

"She took me in after my family died. Showed me a better and enjoyable life. And as I grew older with her by my side, I grew closer and closer to her. Until the day that she..." Mr. Crusader could not bring himself to say anymore.

"So you taught yourself to shoot and became a mercenary." Davis continued.

"Pretty much. I needed to pay the bills somehow and it wasn't like I had any qualifications." Mr. Crusader said. "What about you?"

"Me? Well... my life is a bit dull compared to yours Major. I was born not too far from here actually. About ten miles north of Dallas. My parents moved us further east after that.

I grew up with a normal family in a normal home. Went to school and got good grades. Even met a girl there, married her a few years later.

I got a job in textiles and then moved onto science. Worked in an observatory for a while before pushing my way into what I thought was a research department owned by FEMA." Davis explained.

"I'm guessing that it wasn't owned by FEMA then?" Mr. Crusader asked.

"No. Instead it turned out to be Sector Eighteen of the SCD. After they hired me, I learnt that FEMA didn't even exist. It was just a public cover for SCD operations. So you see, I'm here by choice. Nothing special about that." Davis said with a smile.

"Kids?" Mr. Crusader asked.

"Closest I ever came was a dog. He passed a few years back though."

"Sorry." Mr. Crusader told him.

"He was old, it was sad but it couldn't be helped. Thirteen was a good age for a husky I suppose." Davis told him.

"What's your clearance level again?" Mr. Crusader asked Davis quietly as to not be overheard by the men standing guard on the other side of the door.

"Ten." Davis said in confusion.

"So what secrets are waiting for me at ten? I'm only an eight." Mr. Crusader asked, realising that since his sudden promotion he had yet to undergo a fresh top secret briefing on everything that he was allowed to know now that he was a major.

"You know I shouldn't." Davis said.

"Just one thing then." Mr. Crusader whispered. "The SCD has a mage on their side, they have to. Someone who moves about freely and is trusted. That's the only way that I can explain all of the advances that we have made in the past decade. So who is it?"

"I don't know. I've never met him but I know of him. Everyone calls him a genius but I think that he's just better informed than we are. The only thing that I do know about him is that he isn't just trusted. He's an employee. He has an agent ID and living quarters. Has done for as far back as the records go." Davis told Mr. Crusader in a hushed voice.

"Right then." Mr. Crusader said quickly, perking up almost instantaneously as he decided that a change of pace would be the perfect way to pass the time whilst his medication and alcohol wore off. "Kitchen?"

"Yeah it's just down the hall. We should be fine from that

distance." Davis said as he stood himself back up, watching as Mr. Crusader went to do the same.

At least, that was the plan.

Instead though, the ring once again, took matters into its own hands.

Mr. Crusader's sudden decision to leave his close proximity to the ring prompted it to act. And act it did.

The ring appeared on Mr. Crusader's finger by means of a self-activated teleport to his person upon sensing his intention to leave and the next thing that Mr. Crusader knew, was cold.

Dreadful wind and unwavering cold.

The ring having teleported him out of the facility and far away from all civilization that he knew to distance both itself and him from the SCD. The funny thing was however, that where he landed was almost exactly where he needed to be.

It wasn't as though he or the ring had known to go there but where he found himself now was sat at the foot of a snow covered mountain.

On the northern border of Nepal.

"What?" Mr. Crusader questioned fiercely as he stood himself back up.

The ring on his finger, was surprisingly quick to respond.

"You made a promise to slay that dragon, as is your duty. This seemed like as safe a place as any to do it." The voices told him.

And with nothing but snow and dirt in all directions, Mr. Crusader didn't have a choice. He was stuck, with no way of getting back but in the end, he wouldn't need to.

"This is Mordoa." The General said as he answered the ringing phone being placed in his hand by a young officer approaching him.

"It's Davis sir. Major Crusader and the ring are gone, teleported from what I can tell." He reported, and having already waited twenty minutes it was about time too.

"Do we know where?" The General asked in subdued rage.

"It was a simple matter of reconfiguring our satellites. And sir, you won't believe where he landed."

It would seem that General Mordoa would have to speed up the plan. Forgetting the plane and going for the fastest option that he had.

It was a good idea to bring the dolls after all. He would have never made it in time if he hadn't.

THE LAST DRAGON SLAYER

15
A SWIFT END

Nepal. A cold and isolated place. Thwart with mountains and snow. Offering little in resources and fertile land and yet still populated heavily by humanity.

The rabbits that they are had spread out wide in their early years but still found themselves packed in together by the end. But luckily for Mr. Crusader, that population was far from his position. So far in fact, that they would have been hard pressed to perceive the conflict that was about to begin even if there hadn't been a snowstorm surrounding him.

The chilling crisp to the air grabbing at his flesh and sinking in within seconds. The snow building up on his hair and shoes almost instantly. The moisture in the breath that exited his lungs freezing upon contact with the air. And the slight feeling of numbness from his alcohol and morphine vanished entirely as the cold created a numbing sensation of its own.

He wasn't going to last long in that state. And he knew it.

But that came later.

He thought himself all alone when he arrived. And whilst true a few stray members of society might have been on the mountain pass to the east of him – perhaps even in tents or hidden in caves to wait out the storm as its severity worsened – it was unlikely that such a small number would have ever been believed had they seen anything that morning.

From the white flakes of ice falling from the sky to the frozen trees surrounding their positions, there was no chance of then securing a clear line of sight to the conflict to come. And even if they had, they would have been far more likely to die from the fallout just from being close enough to see it in the first place.

Mr. Crusader had little to worry about in the way of witnesses, not that such a concern was his top priority at the time however.

An SCD employee – an officer – he might have been; a stickler for their rules and regulations he was not.

Going against protocol was a common occurrence for him. Skipping over the requirement to scout out and secure an area before conducting any operation be it sanctioned or not was a thought that never even had to cross his mind.

He just did it automatically.

More to the point however. When he arrived there, his thoughts were focused on one thing and one thing alone.

Where the hell was he?

As far as he knew, he had been sat on the floor of the decontamination checkpoint before entering secured storage when he had just disappeared. The next thing that he could see was snow and a lot of it.

Having never been though a teleport before, not being personally familiar with the experience, he had been yet to make that connection either.

At the time, he might well have believed anything that anyone told him about how he got to his location or where that even was for that matter. Even if he had been told that it was all a dream or vision, he would have believed that too.

But as he came to the conclusion that his feeling of cold was real and that so too must have been his surroundings, he accepted that he had been moved. He did not understand why such a place had been chosen though.

'Of all the places to take me why choose one so cold?' He

thought.

It wasn't long after this thought that his answers would come however. Because as luck, fate or just good timing would have it, the ring now almost permanently bound to him and his finger had chosen that moment to begin its explanation to him. It had sensed enough confusion by then to have already decided that its master wasn't going to figure out the rest by himself.

But first, there was the matter of heat to deal with. Or at least, the lack of it. Freezing temperatures and lightly dressed humans do not always go well together.

And as Mr. Crusader began to shiver, clenching his hands together tightly and watching as his breath moved through the air around him, all of that suddenly changed.

A slight spring was felt in his step, an increase in endurance and also in strength as well. His hands tighter than they had ever been and his mind wide awake also.

His intoxication from alcohol was gone, his high from the morphine as well. His head made clearer and his body more energised than it had ever been before. All of his senses had been completely altered, heightened. In addition his body was strengthened and his feeling of cold rid from his perception completely as well.

Mr. Crusader was either starting to trip or something had changed in him. It did not take long for something to answer that question for him though.

"Better?" The child like voices of the ring asked him in a tone far more calm than they had spoken to him before.

"I feel so light... and warm. What did you do?" Mr. Crusader asked it in amazement at his newfound strength. Smiling as he lightly hopped on each leg.

"You are to do battle soon. It made sense to prepare your body for it." The voices told him. "Agility, endurance, strength and resistance to the elements to name but a few of the improvements that your power now offers you have been activated."

"You can do all that?" Mr. Crusader asked it.

"No, I cannot. You can. I merely took the liberty of implanting the idea in your mind and went from there." The ring explained.

"Cleaver." He muttered.

"I do not have an intellect, just a set amount of responses to certain stimuli. You are about to do battle and were not prepared. My actions rectified that." It told him.

"Sorry but I have to ask this; it's been bothering me for a while now. What exactly are you?" Mr. Crusader questioned as he stared down at the ring lightly glowing against the white haze of the snow on his hand.

"You mean to ask of my intelligence, my consciousness? Am I a life form or simply a machine?" It asked him.

"Yes." He said, nodding as he did so.

"I am not a person, not as you would describe the term. But I'm not a life form, nor am I a machine. All I am is all I have ever been. A tool built from ancient materials for the sole purpose of slaying dragons. And once that purpose is fulfilled and the last of them dead, I will depart." It explained to him.

"Depart?" He asked.

"With no purpose my reason for being becomes moot. I shall rip my consciousness from this vessel and allow it vanish. Or die, as humans might put it." The ring explained.

"So when we are done here?" Mr. Crusader asked.

"We?"

"Like it or not you have a level consciousness that is high enough to hold complex conversations and you a voice. It is a far easier to talk to you as I would another than it is to focus on changing my use of language." Mr. Crusader said.

"I do not have a problem or distaste with your use of language master, I am merely shocked with your choice to work with me. Up until now trusting you has been... trying." The voice said.

"That was when I was still under the supervision of the SCD. With none of them here I am able to do as I wish. This includes getting this Dragon Slayer business over with so that I can go back to how things were." He told it.

"Then to go back to your previous question. When we are done here, the dragon shall be dead and I shall be gone. My purpose complete and your destiny fulfilled." It said.

"Destiny?" Mr. Crusader questioned, taking issue with the use of the word from an atheist's point of view. He never had been one to believe in a higher power, or fate. His life was his own to live, as it should have been.

"As a creature born of magic, I have the ability to *hear* certain things. The story of your tale, is well known to me. It was not until now that I realised the connection but if *we* go through with this then it will come to pass. And you will become the very last of the Dragon Slayers. The one destined to exterminate their entire species." The ring explained somewhat cryptically.

"So you can see the future, that's what you're telling me?" Mr. Crusader asked sarcastically.

"Not so much see as it is peek. I hear bits and pieces over time. Most do not make sense, others are unrelated to me or my purpose but a few of them were of you master. I pieced the story together some time ago. It is only now that I understand what it meant." The ring said.

"So you're telling me that it was predestined for me to wear this ting and kill this dragon?" He asked.

"Not specifically but someone saw this end coming a long time ago and that sight sent the events fracturing across the world though the great network of mana that surrounds us. It was not me that made this prediction, I merely heard of it." The ring tried to tell Mr. Crusader but he stopped paying any real attention to the words that were spoken to him after his destiny was initially mentioned.

He didn't really care.

"So nothing can go wrong then? Good." Mr. Crusader grinned, clenching his right fist and watching as the jewel of the ring began to glow vibrantly in response to his tense state.

As far as he was concerned he had just been told that he was going to win. That was all he needed to hear. Now he was ready for a fight.

"That isn't exactly what I..."

"So do you have a name?" Mr. Crusader asked it suddenly.

"Why would I?"

"I assume that you have communicated with your masters in the past yes?" Mr. Crusader asked.

"Not this intimately or for as prolonged a time but yes. It has happened on occasion." It said.

"Then what did they call you?" He asked it.

"Asra, fifth of the elder stones. That was the name that I was always referred to by but never directly called. The man who would have given it to me didn't live long enough to get the chance. But I saw the thought in his mind during my service to him, I knew regardless of his silence." The ring told him.

"You can see my thoughts too then?" Mr. Crusader asked somewhat defensively.

"Not your deeper emotions or memories, just your immediate intentions and plans. The thoughts of the moment so to speak." The ring explained.

"Well Asra, how do we do this then?" He asked quickly, changing the topic whilst throwing in a change in the way that he addressed the tool on his finger as well.

"I believe that summoning the dragon would be the best place to start. However first..."

"Actually you should probably tell me where we are?" Mr. Crusader asked quickly, trying to at least understand some of the situation before him.

"I believe that in your modern tongue this place is referred to as Nepal. Beyond that I am not sure." Asra told him.

"Why?" Mr. Crusader asked impatiently.

"It was the first place that came to me, I'm not sure why."

Asra explained.

"Okay, continue what you were saying." Mr. Crusader told it.

"Of course. I recommend transforming your arms beforehand. It is not something that can be done for you if you forget and you may not get a chance after the dragon arrives." Asra said.

"My arms? Into blades you mean?" Mr. Crusader asked.

"They are the only weapons in your arsenal that can actually kill a dragon. The rest of your abilities can only wound and subdue it." Asra explained to him.

"So I just think about it right, imagine it happening?" He asked, concentrating after the fact and then watching as both his right and left arms were transformed into three foot long blades extending from his elbow.

Both of them tearing their way through the sleeves of his fresh shirt as it happened. The excessive build-up of heat along the metallic edge of the weapons becoming visible as they reacted to the cold temperature of the air.

They were tinted purple and connected directly to the bone. More powerful than most other blades and formed from a material that no human technology would have been able to break. Or quantify for that matter.

The perfect weapons... for Dragon Slayers anyway.

"These blades were what gave my first master and his brethren the upper hand in the purge. Allowing them not only to withstand the great force of the attacks that they received but to be able to repay them tenfold.

Without these, we would have never won." Asra recounted.

"It feels weird. Like my hands are just fixed in one position even though I know they're not there anymore... I will be able to turn back at will when this is over right?" Mr. Crusader asked.

"In all the time between my forging and now, never has a slayer been unable to revert their hands back to normal without dying first. Even when broken or cut from the body, the hand should return. In the same shape as the blade though." Asra explained quickly as to hide the severity of the risks involved.

"Good." Mr. Crusader grinned.

"I will begin opening the void now." The ring said, a bright red light shining through the metal now in place of where the ring would have been on his finger and continuing to increase in power by the second.

Within a minute of charging, the portal had appeared. A black spiral of energy swirling around and around like a vortex in mid-air. Hovering many meters off of the ground and expanding ever so slightly with every second.

Then the centre of this vortex turned to pitch black, a puddle of almost liquid black that expanded to cover the entire thing before long. And through it moments later, came a talon.

Followed by four more and the foot connecting them. Then the leg and the beginning of the upper body before finally the head pierced through as well.

The dragon, stepping into the real world in a permanent form for the first time in over one thousand years. That would have been cause for celebration, had he not done it knowing that it would lead to his death.

But as its tail passed through the portal as well, it vanished and at last the dragon that had been locked inside of its void cage for many generations was finally free.

Stretching out its wings and neck to enjoy the fresh air before finally looking down to the small speck of biological matter known as a human standing before him.

"Young Slayer. I thank you." It told him.

"Telos-Urin... I'm not sure how to greet someone that I intend to kill. It's not like we're friends or anything." Mr. Crusader said loudly in confusion.

"Then if enemies we must be I assume that you have come prepared? Even if I am to die, I still wish to go out fighting. As all those who dies to protect me did as well." It said.

"As would many in your position." Mr. Crusader told it.

Then silence filled the air. The dragon looking to the sky above him and then the ground below and thinking over its decision. Trying its hardest to recognise his location but failing completely as his memory did the same.

He found himself lost in that moment. Unable to recognise the world that he had returned to and unable to justify his choice to fight to his death.

He no longer had anything that he could fight for. Nothing that killing Mr. Crusader would avenge.

In fact he had nothing at all.

No dreams that could become reality even if he were to try and make them so and no desire to continue on with his pointless existence.

So when the dragon turned back to Mr. Crusader standing cautiously below him, he changed his mind.

"But even so. To feel the wind in my wings once more, the cold and the dirt, it is already more than enough to make me overlook that. Perhaps for your sake, I can allow you to kill me with ease. There isn't much for me to fight for after all." It told him.

"Are you sure?" Mr. Crusader asked.

"Yes. Yes I am sure. I shall die by your hand, that is decided. Now make it quick Slayer, I have no intention of experiencing pain in my final moments." The beast explained, dropping his head and looking to the floor to expose the rear of its neck to Mr. Crusader, placing it well within striking distance.

"So how do I do this?" Mr. Crusader whispered to the ring.

"The base of my skull, where the scales of my neck are at their thinnest is the weakest and most lethal place that a Slayer can strike. One deep slash across their and I will be dead in moments. I would ask that you do not take your time Slayer. My happiness will not outlast my will to live forever." The dragon told him.

"What of the heart that you mentioned earlier?" Mr. Crusader pointed out.

"A surer way of killing me it may be but a pain free one it is not. Your blade though my spinal cord will be enough. It will just take longer for my body to give up trying to heal me after the fact." The dragon explained dimly, accepting the reality of the words it was saying.

"Alright then." Mr. Crusader said.

He leant down, positioning his legs accordingly and readying himself for the jump. Breathing in deeply and making sure his aim was precise and that his arms were ready to move.

And within a few moments, he jumped.

Leaping from the floor with such force that an indent was left in it many metres across like the shockwave from a grenade going off at his feet. Blasting him towards the dragon at speeds not too dissimilar to that of the rail guns that he had encountered before and shooting him at his target with deadly precision.

He moved his arms into position as he neared the neck, ready to swing them at a moment's notice but at the same time, he heard something. A terribly loud sound like crackling thunder at the same time as an explosion.

And as Mr. Crusader instinctively turned to look, it was already too late.

Even as he tried to move his arms into position to deflect the blast, it still hit him.

The full force of a beam of bright red heat, like a laser or breath of fire. And it sent him flying within an instant.

The only one left to see what had happened was the dragon that he had left behind and he was as confused in that moment as it was possible to be.

For standing before him, having just landed after soaring down from the sky above, was the last thing that he ever thought he would see.

Another dragon.

But not just any dragon. As it was imprinted on him at a

young age, there was no mistaking it even after all their time apart. That dragon; was his father.

And judging by its size and most certainly its age and power, there was no doubting it. In his time since Telos had last seen him, he had become not only an Elder but a fully matured Arch Dragon as well.

More deadly than anything a single Dragon Slayer had faced before and seemingly now with an ally as well.

Mr. Crusader didn't have a chance.

But for him to realise that, he would have to get back up first.

THE LAST DRAGON SLAYER

16
MAY BATTLE COMMENCE

The skies above beckoned. The clouds tore apart and the light of the morning sun above shone through the gaping hole brightly, piercing the intense winds and snow filled air and reaching down; touching the dirt and rock beneath. Revealing it from its flaked white cloak for but an instant as it came. The event followed.

Where once it had appeared as though the heavens themselves had opened to quell the storm through which they had pierced, now seemed far more like the reverse.

Heaven did not open its gates then; hell did. And through its gates came something far darker than any could have imagined. Dark enough, to have even intensified the storm upon its arrival.

The crackling sound of lightless thunder, the roaring sound of heatless fire enveloped the air as it shot down to the ground below as he drew ever closer.

Then a crash, louder and stronger than anything ever heard before as he collided with the ice and snow beneath him. The ground heaving, his force impacting and denting it as he landed. A permanent landmark, to remember his arrival that day.

Then the clouds snapped back into position, covering the sun entirely and returning the landscape to that of the cold winter storm that it had been before. The light dim and the atmosphere growing ever darker as the milliseconds ticked by.

Where once there had been a powerful snow storm both harsh and enduring, there was now something far worse hidden within it. A dark presence with malice in its intent and rage in its veins lurking within the rough visibility of that moment.

Obscured by the landscape in part at first, then the dust and dirt that had been thrown up from its landing and then finally by the darkness and snow that surrounding him not a moment later.

To anyone who hadn't been looking, he was invisible. Surprising when he had been adamant on making an entrance for himself. He had been planning that reunion for a while. He was not about to pass up the opportunity to show off.

Or in reality; he wasn't about to allow the opportunity for his opponent to gain the upper hand to exist. It was strike first or be struck upon. And he had already decided which one he would chose long before he arrived that day.

Because for the first time in over a millennium, both he and the last of the dragon slaying rings, could meet face to face. But for the first time; it would be on far more equal terms.

Towering over the peaks of the hills with great prowess and unmistakable dominance as he made himself known to the others. Opening his jaws wide and unleashing the raging torment contained deep within.

A light of brilliance radiated out of him. A laser of heat and fire – energy more powerful than anything that he or the ring had been built or expected to withstand – and it was racing towards Mr. Crusader as he flew through the air by the nanosecond.

Barely even giving him the chance to see it coming.

The air went uncomfortably still in that moment, the sound went way down low as though it were being dimmed and the world all but stopped moving as this beam of energy made contact with the young Slayer. His death surly approaching soon after it.

A dragon's breath far more powerful than any that he or his

kind had faced before had been fired with success and aimed precisely to meet its mark. There was no doubting it, it was going to it. And then as it did, as the next moment came to pass; he was gone. Vanishing from sight almost entirely as he ventured off into the distant snow.

Mr. Crusader being instantly thrown out of sight as the great and unchallengeable force of the beam hit him head on. Sending him flying just as he had been before that moment at tremendous speeds into the snow covered distance and out of mind within an instant. For as he left the scene, the other one entered it.

A deep red hue covering its exterior from top to bottom. Painting the many thousands of individual scales and the soft hide protected beneath without any slight hint of an end.

Deep and lifeless black eyes whose cold stare sent a powerful and unmistakeable shiver down the spine of the one left looking upon them.

A white line following the left side of its face from jaw to neck forming the scar that he now wore. The mark left to him by the one who had ultimately been incapable of killing him. The one for which Mr. Crusader had to thank for his current pain and predicament.

Had he been stronger, or perhaps even a little smarter, that beast would have been dead long ago and Mr. Crusader might have been able to do his deed with a little peace. But as fate would have it, that dragon survived the conflict that claimed the life of the strongest Dragon Slayer to ever live.

Leaving it free and dormant to encroach on Mr. Crusader when his time finally came to wear the same ring. Not knowing of the unbreakable tie between it and the monster now attacking its new and inexperienced master.

It had yellow teeth that were both sharp and chipped filling its mouth from end to end that were made visible as it took each laboured breath. A strong limp on its hind left side form an ancient injury that was allowed to heal on its own before mana could even be considered.

The after effects of a bone that was once fractured badly enough to have severed nerves. Then walked on and forced through use for months as he endured the pain in order to survive the endless array of battles that were ahead of him. Dedicating his mana to his attacks and defences and neglecting his leg for as long as he could.

Finally leaving it in a state that was irreparable by his powers, cursing him to limp for the rest of his life. However short that was expected to have been.

And with wings so large that they blocked out the sun, the wind and the snow falling from above once risen with enough force; it was clear to see that its life had been a long and enduring one.

Both were almost completely covered in small rips and tears, cuts from battle impossible to mend fully and instead forming into permanent features of its body.

Neither scars nor wounds, they were somewhere between and from the state that each of them were in – red with soreness and swelling around the edges ever so slightly – it was reasonable to assume that they were quite painful to live with.

Then a misshapen tail extending from his rear, bulged near the tip and snake like in form. Damaged from its many battles and injuries but still attached to the body; an appendage that the beast would have preferred existing without due to its condition.

And a back whose spikes ran deep. Rooting from the bone and extruding upwards for almost two meters at times, they were razor sharp and harder than steel.

Everything about him shouted the same thing to any who would have dared to look upon such a frightening visage.

That he was not under any circumstances, to be fucked with.

However, for Telos-Urin, the dragon stood before him that was far younger, smaller and weaker than the one that he was looking at in terror, it didn't matter.

That cold hard stare might not have been one that he recognised but that smell and that power was.

There was no doubt in his mind that it was him. And as the two made eye contact, looking to one another for many moments as they both sussed up the other, that recognised connection between them seemed to have been mutual.

Telos lowered his head and entire body in submission. Recognising the power that this elder dragon possessed and respecting it. Taking no chances when it came to interacting with this beast as to remain as safe as he could in his presence.

But something seemed wrong almost instantly as he did so.

The dragon that looked at him, that stared down upon the weakling at his feet with a hateful glare holding both rage and ill intent behind its veil; made no attempt to communicate with him.

Dragons being a species far older and far more in tune to magic had the innate ability to communicate through their own version of telepathy. Incompatible with the brainwaves of humans and far superior to any form of verbal speech and yet, both minds remained silent.

Even though distance was a minute factor, at such a close proximity they should have been able to sense each other at the very least. But for Telos, he sensed absolutely nothing.

No thoughts and no will. No attempt to make any communication with him beyond that of the stare that he already wore.

But it was far more than that.

The mana coming from him, the black aura surrounding his body in its entirety, was foreign to Telos. Not that of the father he once knew and not that of any other dragon either.

So foreign in fact, that to the best of his knowledge it was the first time that he had come across it.

And as this dragon drew closer to him, inspecting him from end to end as his eyes moved left to right, he could taste it entering his mouth. The foul air surrounding him and everything else as it poured out of this beast. The sickening black stench that was seemingly excreting from him. And it caused him to feel fear.

It was unlike any form of mana that he had ever seen before and for good reason. Because depending on the description, it wasn't strictly speaking a form of mana. This was corruption. Pure and unfiltered. Straight from the original source and without any alteration or deterioration. Powerful black mana that absorbed all others that it touched.

And it was fused with him.

Whatever that thing was that was approaching Telos in that moment, it was neither natural nor was it a father. Not anymore.

And as Telos began to realise that, what happened next made it all the more obvious that this would not be the reunion that he had hoped for upon recognition of the dragon nearing him. Because as soon as it was close enough, this dragon, took a bite at him.

Throwing his head down towards the back of Telos's and clamping down with its jaws.

Had it not been for the surprisingly resilient Dragon Slayer impaling this new dragon in the face as it drew closer to the neck of Telos, he would have been dead almost instantly.

The dragon had been aiming for his weakest point. The very same one that only moments ago Telos had been telling Mr. Crusader about.

The dragon flinched in pain after the attack. Telos jumped back to a safe distance instinctively as he realised the danger that he was in and from there the standoff began.

From there, the battle that one way or another would end either the Dragon Slayers or the dragons themselves would ultimately commence.

Mr. Crusader, who had since his short disappearance figured out how to master his new teleportation abilities, jumped down from the beast and landed next to Telos. Seeing him as a temporary ally in that fight at the very least and deciding to side with him until it was over.

Even in his naivety, he knew that he didn't stand a chance against this new opponent alone. But then again, his odds weren't that well improved even with the help. But he wasn't able to see that at the time. He still had much more to learn.

"I take it that I can kill this one as well?" Mr. Crusader asked quickly upon landing by Telos's side.

"Slayer remain here. I WILL HANDLE THIS MYSELF!" He replied forcefully, stepping out in front of Mr. Crusader and positioning himself between his father and the infant Slayer behind him.

He still needed someone capable of ending his life to do the deed when he was done with that fight. Not that he actually believed that he had a chance of winning either though.

"You sure?" Mr. Crusader questioned, recognising the obvious power gap between the two.

"This is my father!" Telos shouted, butting heads with the dragon that he faced, literally, only a moment later. "No matter what state he is in now…"

The dragon pushed Telos back, reaching down to bite at his lower neck. But the right leg of Telos raised quickly, swiping at this dragon and impacting it with such force that it was thrown back to the left.

Once there and at a far enough distance, Telos's mouth opened, an orange glow quickly being emitted by it as he prepared himself for the taxing process of breathing such powerful mana.

"He is still my responsibility!" Telos shouted once more, breathing a beam of fire far wider than he had done before, grazing the neck of his father and then running along his left side as it continued.

Smashing into the scales and burning through right down to the hide. Scorching the body and burrowing deep into the flesh. But it did not last long.

This dragon had been through far worse than that before and

had come out on top, it knew how to survive, how to fight. And against one of his own, it knew that the slightest nock would easily turn the tides when the other was distracted.

And as the tail of the dragon came flying through the air it soon collided with the head of Telos, sending his beam off course and providing an opening for attack as he desperately tried to reposition it.

The dragon, now dripping with blood all the way down its left side as the cut made by that beam slowly healed itself pounced at Telos.

Jaws wide open and teeth sharp. Its front legs raised and prepared to grab at his neck upon contact. And with every ounce of strength that Telos had in that moment placed into the beam that he continued to fire uncontrollably, Mr. Crusader quickly realised that he was not capable of doing this alone.

No matter his wishes, he would have to step in.

Teleporting above the target quickly nearing Telos and then shooting straight down like a bullet. Using basic wind magic to create a bubble of high density air below the bottom of his feet and focusing it on the soles of his shoes as it was released violently. Propelling him towards the dragon with both speed and force. Exactly as he had figured it would.

At least he could think on his feet.

His attack managing to pin the dragon beneath him to the floor and halting his movement for the moment at least as his placed the both of his blades into the right shoulder of the beast and forced it to come smashing down into the ground.

Saving Telos in the process.

The dragon beneath him squealed, unable to move for the moment from the pain alone and as Telos finally stopped the firing of his beam, the time for scolding Mr. Crusader that he had wished to take, quickly passed.

The dragon shot back up violently then, knocking Mr. Crusader off of him and into the air. And as the teeth of this dragon closed in, trying to swallow him whole; his positioning thrown off by his sudden change of location preventing him from teleporting for at least another second, Telos was forced to step in as well.

Moving left swiftly and biting down on the right wing of the dragon, pulling it away from Mr. Crusader just enough that its teeth could not reach him as he recovered from his fall.

And with that wing in his mouth, Mr. Crusader teleported above it, performing the same tactic as before and launching himself straight down. Spinning rapidly as he went, slicing through both bone and flesh with his blades as he ran across the surface of the wing. And with Telos pulling on it already, it tore from the body long before Mr. Crusader ever reached the bottom.

Grounding the beast and severely harming it in the process.

In reaction to the pain it moved to attack yet again.

Clamping its own teeth into the body of Telos, just above the left shoulder in his neck. Grabbing and pulling with force as Telos clawed at his neck and face. Throwing him many metres away as his superior strength allowed him to both lift and launch the dragon in his grasp.

And with Mr. Crusader still picking himself up from his previous attack, unable teleport again in such quick succession from the previous three, all he could do was watch as it happened.

The mouth of the dragon opening, a bright red glow coming out of it and aimed directly towards Telos in the distance. A beam of fire and heat, pure raging mana more powerful than his own, bearing down on him quickly.

And even though Mr. Crusader went through the motion of jumping to intercept it, knowing that his body could survive at least a short expose to its power as it had done the last time, he was too slow.

But that did not mean that he was too late.

Because as the energy began to leave the mouth of this beast, its head quickly jerked to the left unexpectedly. A small fiery explosion occurring on its right before the fact.

An explosion facilitated by the rocket propelled grenade fired from the hills to the east.

A barely visible and much appreciated group of soldiers standing upon it. And as Mr. Crusader saw them, he knew; that there was no chance that he would lose. Not anymore.

And with that, with his body beginning to leave the floor as he jumped to the head of the dragon now beginning to face him after its forced movement to the left, he put everything that he had into fighting.

There was no need not to anymore.

His backup had finally arrived.

After taking so long debating the risks of using the machine dolls in their company to teleport them directly to the target, their timing had been left so perfect; that it almost seemed intentional.

And now that they were there and could see that Mr. Crusader and Telos were fighting this larger dragon, they quickly involved themselves as well.

Their help would be greatly appreciated in due time.

And as he approached the head of the beast; impacting and impaling the lower neck of the dragon, Mr. Crusader's blades dug in deeper with yet another strong push. The blood covering him within an instant as he sliced across it from right to left. A cut that whilst deep, painful and debilitating, was unfortunately not fatal.

Even with all the wounds that he had sustained so far, it had not been enough to keep him down. Not yet.

But with Mr. Crusader quickly approaching the hill that his fellow officers were stood upon with weapons drawing and aimed as he fell through the air still unable to teleport, his glancing strike, was enlarged tenfold.

The spiked tail of Telos swinging through the air and hitting his father in the lower jaw. Forcing his head up and tearing the cut that Mr. Crusader had made open even further.

Then as the weak point became clear, the weapons that the soldiers had brought with them launched their attack as well.

Three of them as planned. Machine dolls, magic in origin but entirely human by design. Shaped in the form of a basic bipedal creature but with plastic like skin and no personalisation to distinguish one from the other. They were almost robotic. And as they stood up from their prone positions in the snow and abandoned the last of the rail guns that they had carried, they each disappeared.

Teleporting to the throat of this beast and carrying out the orders that had only just moments ago been given to them. Clamping their hands around the cut and holding themselves close as they performed the act.

Self-detonation.

The mana crystals within them pooling with power and expanding rapidly as they drew closer to cataclysmic collapse. Heat building up in them and beginning to melt their bodies before the light of their power began radiating out of them.

Three bright blue lights shining for the shortest of moments before fire replaced them.

An implosion of brilliant power occurred next. An almost liquid form of mana surrounding the dolls like a bubble before collapse. The resulting explosion that followed blasting apart scales, bone and flesh as it tore through the dragon. Leaving a gaping hole in the lower neck and upper chest where most of its body had once been.

And as this beast reacted to the pain, barely even able to move as the Corruption forced its now obviously deceased body to move, Telos made one final attack.

Clamping down with his jaws onto the upper neck of the dragon just below its chin. Placing his left claw onto the shoulder of the beast as he pulled and pushing down with great force as he continued to do so.

Ripping and tearing at the body until it broke. The bones snapping apart and the arteries severing.

The head decapitated and the rest of the body left to rot as it hung from his mouth.

The remains of the dragon dropped to the floor, Corruption unable to sustain it any further and the eyes of the head slowly closing as the power sustaining its life finally ran out.

His father who had long since passed on finally put to rest as his body died at last.

Telos dropping the head and staring down at it in dread over what he had just done for many moments after this. Bathing in the glory of victory but also in the despair of guilt as he came to realisation of what that victory had entailed. But the time for that soon passed.

Mr. Crusader quickly stood himself back up and looked to the hill where his commanding officer and fellow soldiers stood with a smile as they watched in amazement and then turning back to Telos seconds later.

Turning to him too with the same smile but that smile then quickly turned sour as he saw it. The extent of the damage that he had received.

Blood dripping down from his neck, face and leg.

An obviously broken hind right leg and shattered scales from head to toe.

His face charred and scared permanently. The beam of energy fired at him in fact colliding with him for the briefest of moments as the SCD tried to redirect it. The puncture wounds from the teeth clamping done on his neck exposing muscle and deep tissue beneath the skin.

All of these injuries would have been survivable had they been singular or suffered whilst at full strength but they weren't.

All of that damage and an almost exhausted mana supply had led to one thing. A slow and painful death.

And the blood loss that he had sustained so far, was already far beyond even what a dragon could survive. He should have dropped by then. There wasn't any biological reason as to why he hadn't.

He wasn't going to last much longer. Not without a serious amount of healing magic. Which after such a draining a fight like that – one that had exhausted his mana supply and also Mr. Crusader's – was far removed from the picture.

He was dying. And all that could be done by everyone else, was watch.

The last of the dragons, was beginning to pass on.

The extinction of an entire species, beginning to be observed by those onlookers that stood around him.

Mr. Crusader's destiny, was quickly coming to a close.

THE LAST DRAGON SLAYER

17
FINAL BREATHS

The destiny that had awaited Mr. Crusader for many years had come at last. The fight between the last of the dragons and the last of the Dragon Slayers had begun as the world had known it would for over a millennium.

Mr. Crusader, the last ring bearer and the last descendent of the first Slayers had taken up his fight. Standing beside one of the very beasts that his kind were meant to destroy and helping it in its stand to kill the wretched monster that had emerged in response to its return.

The battle lasted mere minutes. Dishing wounds to both sides and exacting a heavy price both physically and mentally to make it through but just like that; the battle was over.

But even with such a short amount of time for that battle to endure through, the result was the same. One side was defeated and the other made the victors. But victory it seemed, came at a much greater price than any had originally believed.

For whilst no casualties had been initially suffered during the battle except on the enemy side, the one casualty that was suffered on the other side; the one that mattered most, came after it was over.

Mr. Crusader had thought that they had won without losing

anything in return but it would seem that such an assessment, was premature.

He had thought himself victorious, not his side. That in some way that was his win, his battle alone and his achievement. And even though that fight was not his; even though it had been Telos whom had been the one to suffer the first true blow and his battle that he had pushed his way into; in a way he wasn't wrong.

That was his victory. But as for his supposed ally, the dragon that he had helped take down the beast that not only threatened their lives but that of many others as well if they hadn't stopped it together, he was not so lucky.

Mr. Crusader barely had a mark on him but that did not mean that everyone fighting with him could say the same.

His arms returned to their normal form during his long stare to the distance as the maximum entropy of the ring's mana output was reached and with their disappearance, his enhanced senses and endurance went as well.

The cold that surrounded him even then came back to his attention very quickly as they did so. He no longer had any meaningful resistance to the chill of the air that blew past him with force every other instant. He was just as weak as any other human now.

But even so, Mr. Crusader did not have the time to allow himself to shiver. Because just like it was at the age of twelve, hiding under his parents bed as the home invader continued slaughtering the rest of his family; he was frozen.

And whilst he had tried to forget that moment; to push it to the back of his mind and ignore it for as long as he could without fully repressing it; what was happening to him now was not something that he would never be able to shift.

And knowing that, knowing that acting in the same way as he had done at such a young age would lead him down the exact same path; he refused the urge to stop moving. Because something far more import required his attention first.

Watching as Telos held his head lower and lower as his strength diminished to the point of feeling faint alerted him instantly. Observing in great detail as he soon began shaking and then swaying from side to side before finally dropping to the floor entirely as his strength to stand vanished

The snow began to cover him quickly as he planted his body into it; the few flakes in the air that had been blown away from him when he collapsed soon returned as well.

Very soon, be him dead or not, that snow was going to bury him. It was only a matter of time.

Mr. Crusader rushed over to him quickly in response; no longer the same boy that sat idly by as his mother, father, brother and sister were killed by the drunken intruder looking for the cash in their well-stocked family safe, he began sprinting towards the fallen dragon. Knowing that even if he couldn't save him then at least he could make up for his mistake the last time by standing by his side.

He ran right for his head as it laid in the deep snow and dirt and kept going even when the show ran deep enough to reach up his entire leg.

The fresh and soft snow was almost like silk at the time. No time between it settling and that point to allow it to have melted slightly and refrozen into a stronger form of ice it did not have the structure that it needed to support Mr. Crusader's weight. And as he took each step, it covered him even more.

But where Telos had fallen there was now an indent. A crater in the snow where it was thin and harder from the pressure of the creature lying upon it. This allowed Mr. Crusader to pick up speed as his footing improved and make his way to the front of the dragon's head within moments.

His eyes were already beginning to glaze over and his breaths were becoming increasingly slow as Mr. Crusader arrived. And seeing this, the state that he had been left in; made Mr. Crusader realise quite quickly that Telos did not have much longer left to live.

And as the snowstorm around them diminished at last, allowing the both of them to see one another far more clearly than they had been able to do the entire time, those final moments that they shared, began to feel like hours.

"Young Slayer..." Telos sighed weakly. "...Well done."

"Save your strength. I can't kill you if you die." Mr. Crusader said, resting his right hand on the coarse surface of the creature's nose right below his eyes that he stared into deeply.

In response to his feelings and the situation that he faced, the ring on Mr. Crusader's finger activated its final spell quickly. It too was running out of time.

A bright red glow came from it, extending and then surrounding the both of them. Within moments though, it was gone. Everything around them as well.

The world had gone black, the cold was gone as so was the snow. All that was left was Mr. Crusader, Telos and a stranger. A man wearing a suit of armour and carrying his helm under his right shoulder.

It was only when he spoke and when Mr. Crusader looked to the identical ring on his finger that he recognised him.

"You did well... master." He said with a smile. "A corrupt arch dragon and Telos-Urin, the beasts that cost the original and last owners of this ring his life. I am impressed."

"You... the knight that locked him in the void?" Mr. Crusader asked.

"Slayer! Who do you speak with now? My vision is clouded." Telos asked in confusion, barely able to breathe and yet he chose to speak. His sight all but gone by then as well.

The knight approached him and rested his right hand on his head. The ring on his finger glowing brightly and then dimming down again quickly. The eyes of Telos closing, his breaths calming and the pain that he was experiencing vanishing.

"Rest now. Dream of better times..." The knight said, casting a spell with the ring on his finger, or in reality the one on Mr. Crusader's finger and allowing the dragon to believe that in his final moments, he was home.

With his family and the rest of his kind as though the last two thousand years had never happened. And it gave him an immense sense of peace and serenity. Exactly what he had wanted.

"I know that you will have questions. But allow this one to pass first. He is the last of his kind. He deserves respect." The knight told Mr. Crusader as they both looked to the dragon in front of them in an awe filled sadness.

His body was growing colder by the moment, his breaths almost silent and his bleeding beginning to slow as he finally began run out of the blood needed to supply his veins. But even so, even in the face of so much dread, he was happy.

The dream that he was experiencing causing him to smile internally and his eyes to weep their final tears whilst it continued on.

And then within minutes, believing himself to be soaring through the skies above Greenland with his childhood friends, Telos-Urin, the last dragon alive, passed from this world and onto the next.

His species.

Extinct.

"It is done. The last dragon... is dead." The knight said, shedding his own tear before removing his hand and turning to face Mr. Crusader.

"I didn't keep my promise to him!" Mr. Crusader said under his breath as he clenched his fist. Knowing that this event had brought up not only his own emotions but that of the boy that he had once been.

Remembering that in his final talk with his mother he had promised to run. But instead of keeping it he chose to hide in his fear and because of that he felt responsible for their deaths. Because he knew that if he was there the entire time, then he should have tried to save them.

"You might not have granted his spoken wish but you did grant his unspoken one. To return home. And in his final moments, that was where he believed himself to be. You did that." The knight said to him.

"Then I was right, this isn't real?" Mr. Crusader asked.

"No master, it is not." The knight said.

"And by master I assume that you mean..."

"Correct. I am the consciousness of the ring, displayed to you through the last body to wear it before yourself." He said. "As I told you earlier, it is my turn to depart now as well. I thought it best to convene with you in this way before that happened."

"Why? Why do all of this? Taking away his pain and giving him a happy dream in the end, helping me to fight alongside him without resistance. Why do that?" Mr. Crusader asked.

"I was a tool designed to slay them, not to torture or hate them. If they die in the end I have no problem with it. My capability for compassion and cruelty are the same, as long as my purpose is fulfilled." The knight said.

"So now that the last of them is gone?" Mr. Crusader asked.

"As they did, I shall die too. My vessel and its power will still be yours to control but my consciousness will be gone. There will be no further use for it now." The knight explained, the body of the dragon vanishing from view as the world collapsed around the both of them.

"Then that is it? I helped to kill two dragons, using magic far beyond me and now it just ends?" Mr. Crusader questioned.

"I'm afraid so. Your destiny was to slay the last of them, and that is what you did." The knight told him.

"So now?" Mr. Crusader asked.

"I would ask to shake your hand." The knight said.

"But this isn't real?" Mr. Crusader asked.

"But it is to me." He smiled, watching as Mr. Crusader grabbed his extended hand and shook it with force, the both of their rings beginning to glow as they made contact.

And as the black expanse around them disappeared, the knight vanishing entirely as it do so, three final words were heard before the end.

"Thank you. Master."

And with that, it was well and truly over.

Mr. Crusader's ring turned into nothing more than a magical tool and the dragon carcass's beside him began to freeze in the snow. And as that cold set in, as Mr. Crusader began to endure it with General Mordoa quickly marching toward him, the pain took hold.

The extensive damage dealt to his body during that fight, impacting him all at once as the final act of protection by the ring finally wore off. With no consciousness to continuously cast the spell, it collapsed and sent Mr. Crusader into agony once again.

Just as the right hand of the General was to reach his shoulder, he lost consciousness because of it. The General was more than a little confused for a moment but he quickly realised what was wrong after the fact. At the exact moment that the blood began to drool out of his mouth to be precise.

And as the rest of the men rushed over to help, knowing that Mr. Crusader was the only man capable of getting any of them back to the SCD; their tireless effort to save him began.

But as it would happen; they were not as alone as they had believed themselves to be. For up above them, many miles high in the sky; an SCD controlled satellite tasked with tracing a very precise mana signature stopped picking up a signal.

Expecting to find some form of godlike creature based on the readings that they had been monitoring for close to a decade, the troops that were sent in response found the men along with Mr. Crusader and the two deceased dragons there instead.

It turned out that the signature they had been monitoring in its dormant state for all those years had in fact been the arch dragon that Mr. Crusader had just helped to kill.

Luckily for him; by killing it, it sent out a signal that saved his life. His destiny might have been complete but fate wasn't done with him yet. That was clear.

And on the back of a military helicopter headed for the closest SCD run or controlled facility, Mr. Crusader's conflict with the dragons found its end.

The last of the dragons was dead.

The last of the Slayers now without his companion and with that his purpose was complete.

The story was over.

Or at least it seemed to be.

After all, his destiny said that he was to kill the last of the dragons, it did not say that he was to kill the last of the natural ones.

There was still one more to go.

And several months from that moment, after forces under their command managed to capture and then lose the most wanted man in the SCD database, the true destiny of Mr. Crusader revealed itself.

Standing beside the man himself.

The Athereon.

He just didn't know that part yet.

EPILOGUE

Whilst Mr. Crusader laid restless in his bed in the private room given to him on floor nine of the Sector One Eighteen recovery wing – a small outpost on the southern border of China – many more prevalent events continued to occur without him.

In response for the act that he had performed; going above board to uphold the oath that he took to protect and defend the human population of Earth, the newly reformed Council recognised his efforts even though they had not been sanctioned.

This was weeks after the event. Before he had even awoken from the coma that his fight had put him in but nevertheless the proceedings continued without him.

The new Council wanting to make a name for itself by distancing their actions from the previous one as much as they could. Their new members now known by name by none. Given code names and numbers and never seen outside of conference calls.

They very rarely even came within a few dozen meters of each other. The protection and secrecy placed around them was turned up to eleven in light of the events occurring in the magic world.

They were visited by no one but their security staff and unreachable by anyone below the rank of general.

This new council disappeared overnight almost perfectly after it was formed. The only people above them to see to it that their powers were not used immorally or inhumanely remained the Oversight Committee. But like the council, they soon disappeared as well.

It was rumoured for a time that the new members were unlike the previous ones in one crucial way. That they were public figures. Real ones.

It was speculated by some that this new council was comprised of world leaders and politicians in an effort to ensure that the treaties that each nation had signed to give the SCD full authority over everything were being used for a good a just purpose.

If this was in fact the case, then tying any one of these world leaders to the SCD would have surely been made next to impossible. Meaning that even if someone were to suspect another, the likelihood of them being caught before this person was assassinated for their beliefs was exceedingly slim at best.

But in continuation with their efforts to create a new and more trustworthy council capable of overseeing all SCD operations with both absolute authority and no bias towards anything or anyone. This new council was meant to uphold the rules and regulations of the SCD to the letter. To protect and conceal the secret of magic from the rest of the world and to eradicate anything that was inhuman and/or unusable to their cause.

But during their transition to power, it was brought to their attention that Major Timothy Crusader had gone against direct orders and slain the dragon that he had been told would be too risky to go up against. And without any loss of life on the SCD's side as well.

At first the council proposed disciplining the man for his actions but then the full report of what exactly happened in Nepal came through. The tale of how he and the small contingent of troops from the SCD had taken weapons and resources with them to help him in his endeavour.

For the loss of three experimental machine dolls alone those men would have been transferred away from any department that they would have ever been interested in working for but then the council members kept reading.

Learning that through their efforts they had not only taken down the dragon that had been deemed a class one threat but another one as well. One that they had been unknowingly tracking for the better part of a decade as a theorised mage weapon at that.

One that turned out to have been far more powerful and devastating than the already existing threat was in the first place.

The Council soon came to realise; that if Mr. Crusader had not done what he did, then the dragon that he was facing already would have lured in another and that the both of them together would have been far more than the SCD would have ever been capable of handling.

When this council finally learned the full truth based on the reports of the men involved and the statements given by Mr. Crusader before his coma became a factor, they saw it as something no longer worth their reprimand.

Instead, it was something that deserved their immediate compensation.

Seeing his deeds as something far beyond the responsibilities of a Major to handle and promoting him accordingly because of that. Giving him the rank of Lieutenant Colonel along with all pay and security clearance bonus's that came with it.

Then onto the subject of his new powers and abilities, they decided that the best person to lead the team that would be analysing them would be the man himself.

So he was given full and permanent control and full funding of the Cornwall Research Division as well. A command that in the coming weeks of his recovery he took up and even began to enjoy for a time.

This was after waking from his short stay in the coma ward

and only after going through a passing no end of tests and exercises first. The SCD wanted to assess his new found powers in many more ways than one as it seemed.

They needed to know if he was a threat to himself or those around him before he could be trusted. Specifically they wanted to assess his ability to control and understand his powers. To know if he would be able to keep them hidden and not use them unwillingly.

But these tests were all passed with flying colours soon enough. And once he was well enough to travel back to the States by plane, he formally received his briefing on his new position and his new command.

Contained within this file was background information on his new employees and subordinates as well and basic descriptions of their current programs and of the items held in storage at the base.

The last few pages were dedicated to him specifically.

Where he would be living, his new cover and the whereabouts of his much beloved Cadillac that had been seized down the road from the bar that he had originally been found in as well.

And despite the significant change in scenery as well as the sudden change in roles, he soon settled into his new life in Britain shortly after that day.

Finishing the mandatory reading on the files in his hand before formally accepting the position.

There was a small ceremony at Sector Eighteen where he had previously been stationed to say goodbye to him. Not that anyone attending the get together had actually gotten to know him that well expect for those who had been by his side in the weeks leading up to that moment.

Then after that he found himself on a plane; landing in Britain within seven hours and beginning his new life there after that. One that even through wasn't his usual existence, was one that he accepted for the time being.

That was until November of two thousand and seventeen came around at least. Everything changed after that.

Meanwhile though, General Mordoa was given a position close to but not actually on the council at the SCD headquarters hidden beneath the capitol building in Washington.

His new job might not have been that of a councilman as he would have preferred but it was important enough to get him in the same building as one or two of them. Giving him an extra two zero's on his pay check for good measure as well.

Not much is known about what happened to him after that. The first thing that they teach new headquarters personnel is that if they talk, their bodies won't be found.

It is unlikely that General Mordoa ever made contact with anyone outside of his new job after that day. It would have been exceedingly risky to do so.

But with him now sitting at a private desk in his own office down the corridor from the military advisor to the council, the previously known Chairmen Franks, his new power and position did give him both the clearance and the opportunity to do what he had wanted to do for a long time.

Expose the SCD for the inhumane and corrupt organisation that it was.

Above him remained his friend now going by the name of Franks and Franks alone and with him there to make any misdeeds disappear on his behalf as any good friend in power would have done, he got away with his snooping easily.

All of it.

The Oversight Committee made frequent and powerful pushes for increased power over the council after the exposure of Chairwoman Hailey. Taking issue with the way that she had handled matters of planetary defence in previous years specifically and using those as their sole reason to continuously stand up the authority of the Council and push over and over for a more prominent position amongst its members.

Which in the form of their top advisory agent sitting on the council itself, was to everyone's surprise exactly what they received.

And under the new guidance of this mysterious and knowledgeable council member, referring to himself only as the Chronicler, the SCD quickly made magical and technological advancements far beyond what they had done in the past to usher in a new age of worldwide human dominance over magic.

Unknown to most of the members on this new council, both he and the Oversight Committee had quite the ulterior motive to drive them. For not only was this man not to be trusted by humanity; he wasn't even a part of it.

And through his power he set up secret divisions of the SCD to carry out projects of his own off the books. Area's beyond the eye of the Council and reachable only be him.

And it worked.

He took a special interest in Mr. Crusader as it happened. Especially his connection to the void.

He tried tirelessly for months to find a way through himself; even turning to the scientists of the SCD for a time but never making any real progress.

And after it was deemed impossible to reach without the use of Mr. Crusader's ring – whose power had since demised greatly after its consciousness vanished – even that interest which seemed so vital to him, eventually faded.

He was able to explain the rather troubling nature of the dragons' sudden appearance after Telos had come through though. A tale that the rest of the council and the Oversight Committee enjoyed greatly at the time.

He spoke of how this beast had, in his corrupted state, been locked into a perpetual cycle of inactivity between each opening of the Tears.

And with one open at the same time as Telos reappearing, it was only inevitable that he would appear as well. The sensation of another dragon returning after so many years would have certainly gotten his attention.

As for where he had been hiding all of those years or why the SCD had been unable to pinpoint the exact location of the mana signature coming from it that they had been tracking or almost a decade; that was anyone's guess.

But with that said at last, this tale has come to a close.

The last Dragon Slayer now without purpose might well seem like a minor part of the overall story but in the end, he will become far more important than anyone can imagine.

After all, his connection to the void, made him quite the target for the being looking to get there upon his sudden awakening.

The god.

End

The tale of Timothy Crusader continues and concludes in

The Athereon Series
(Starting from "Midnight" onwards)

Printed in Poland
by Amazon Fulfillment
Poland Sp. z o.o., Wrocław